HIVE

Hive

HIVE

by Rachel Starr Thomson

Little Dozen Press

2014

April sat on the shingled roof looking out over the slope of rooftops, the cobbled street, and the bay, watching for the boy. Nick. Her throat burned, and she shivered even though she sat in the sun. A blanket wrapped around her shoulders helped stave off the chill, but the chill came as much from within her body as without, and she knew it. She had flirted far too closely with death only two weeks ago; it wasn't a surprise she was still fighting to get strong.

There he was, slouching around the harbour. He was far, but April had good eyesight. Always had. He walked like he carried too much for a kid his age, maybe eleven. After what had happened with her, she was almost surprised he would go back down there, hang out by the same fishing shack. But then again, she knew a little of what his home life was like, so maybe her being kidnapped by a couple of thugs hadn't actually scared him that much.

She smiled as she thought about his last contact with the

Oneness, the supernatural organism to which April belonged: he had tipped off Tyler and Chris about her abduction. He had done it, April knew, because the Oneness was calling him. He was supposed to become one of them. He just didn't know it yet.

Shoot, she didn't think he knew they existed yet.

She swallowed in frustration, ignoring the raw burn in her throat as she did. She was supposed to be the one reaching out to him, but she hadn't entirely recovered her ability to walk in a straight line.

Which was definitely one reason she was going to get in trouble for sitting on the roof.

"April!" It was Mary, right on time. Slightly harried and definitely concerned. The window beside April creaked open and Mary stuck her head out, forehead creased, and said "April" again in a slightly less startling tone. Probably worried that if she scared April, she would fall.

"I'm okay," April said, turning her head to take in the sight of the older woman climbing gingerly out to sit beside her. "Just watching."

"The boy again?"

"Yes."

"We'll get to him in time. You will."

April sighed. "I already feel late."

"You were trying." Mary's voice was gentle. "You didn't choose what happened. But it was part of the plan. You know that."

April harrumphed. "He needs us. Look at him. No kid should walk like that."

 Rachel Starr Thomson

Mary squinted in the direction of the harbour. "I can't see that far."

"Well, he walks like a little old man. Like . . ."

Mary laid a hand on April's shoulder. "You'll get to him."

Despite herself, April felt the tension ebbing at Mary's touch. There was a reason Mary was the head of this cell. She was wise, and peaceful, a mother even though, like so many of the Oneness, she had never married. Mary moved closer, and April allowed herself to rest her head on her shoulder.

"It's all right," Mary said. "You are recovering. That battle will wait for you. I'm sure of it."

April grimaced, but she kept her eyes closed and nestled further into Mary's shoulder, letting the connection between them settle her heart even more deeply. Battles did not generally wait. But it was good that this one would. The last fight had nearly killed her, and she knew it.

"I'm going for him as soon as I can," she murmured.

"Of course you are," Mary whispered back.

And she would.

* * * * *

It was almost noon when Chris Sawyer walked into his little cottage high up on the cliff, grabbed the sword from over the mantel, and smashed something with it. This time the "something" was an old vase neither of the boys cared about, one nobody cared about, really.

For all that he was making statements, Chris wouldn't have

broken anything that would really hurt anyone else to break.

Aggravated, with himself and with the inconsequential nature of the vase, he put the claymore back up on its hooks and set about picking up the broken pieces of glass with his big hands.

Tyler was sitting in the kitchen, looking over the short counter at the mess in the living room and his friend meticulously tidying it. "Bad day?" he asked.

He winced and regretted the words immediately. He knew full well what the problem with Chris was.

Him.

Or more accurately, the Oneness.

Even more accurately, that Tyler had gone over to the Oneness. At the same Diane, Chris's mother, had finally started to admit she was part of them and they of her. At the same time Reese had almost been destroyed by the Oneness and yet had cemented her unbreakable commitment to them, all at the same time Chris was falling in love with Reese.

Tyler could remember just enough of his own mind and heart before the Joining to know that Chris was in an agony of confusion and resistance and just not understanding. He couldn't blame him.

Of course, if he could only get him to see . . .

He chided himself and stopped there. They'd already had that conversation, and it had already gone badly, enough times. Some things you just had to come to on your own.

On your own.

Three words that Tyler hardly had a context for anymore.

     Rachel Starr Thomson

Chris's voice was tight. "You know what kind of day I'm having."

"Yeah."

"Have you seen Reese?"

"Down by the bay. I said she could take one of the boats out."

Chris yelled. He had closed his hand over a shard of glass without thinking. As he charged into the kitchen to find something to stanch the bleeding, Tyler watched him and wished he could do something, anything, to ease the torment in his friend's soul.

"Have you heard from Richard and Mary?" Chris asked.

"No."

"How long are you going to wait?" Chris asked the question like it was a freight engine, carrying about two hundred cars behind it. "You have to go after the hive!"

"I don't know," Tyler said. He had to admit to some impatience even on his part when it came to that—but he was still so caught up in the euphoria of Joining that he couldn't bring himself to actually cross the line to frustration with the cell leaders. Anyway, he had seen them in action enough to know they were trustworthy. And he had seen the enemy in action enough to know he didn't stand a chance without their full help behind him.

Of course, Chris had seen that too, which was at least partially why he was pacing the cottage and smashing things instead of out trying to rid the world of the creatures who had ripped out Reese's heart and then nearly killed her.

Chris was not Oneness, and he had, he said, no intention of becoming One. But he had every intention of fighting on their side. He had seen the enemy, and he wanted nothing more than to drive that filth out of the world. It wasn't just the demons—though they were terrifying, and horrific. It was the people attached to them. People who weren't born evil through and through, people who had chosen their own depravity. Tyler shuddered.

How many were there, he wondered? People who had been pulled into David's schemes?

Twenty?

A hundred?

A thousand?

Richard wouldn't give numbers. He just said there was a hive, and it was likely very bad. And then he locked himself up with no food or water and prayed, because that was how Richard found power enough to fight demons, by making himself weak and light-headed enough that his head could actually clear and his strength could start to come from some other place.

Tyler, new to all this, didn't try too hard to figure it out. He would wait on their leadership.

The one thing that was not in question was that they were going to fight. They had discovered the hive by no accident. They had attacked its core and exposed its leader. It was a threat, not just to them in some personal way, but to the world. And the Oneness, as Mary had reminded him only last night when they sat at the cell house and looked out over the town's lights and reflections off the water, existed to serve and to save the world.

In the rush of companionship, of love, of profound not-

      Rachel Starr Thomson

aloneness that came with being One, it was almost easy to forget that.

You're a newbie, Tyler reminded himself. It might not always feel this good. It might die away. Get old.

But he remembered how broken, how destroyed Reese had been when she first came and opened his world to the realities of the Oneness. They had fished her out of the water when she tried to drown herself because she believed she had been exiled from the Oneness. Apparently nothing about being One had worn off for her, had dulled or gotten less important. If anything, time had only strengthened the bonds.

From where he sat now, that looked to Tyler like a very, very good thing.

Chris came back from the bathroom with his hand wrapped. "Have you heard anything more about that kid?"

"We're watching him, apparently," Tyler said. "April wants to go after him, but she's still too weak."

He closed his eyes as he spoke. He could feel April, out there somewhere not too far away. Could feel her heartbeat and the way her skin burned and her throat ached. Could feel how much she wanted to get to that boy—the kid she watched and hung out with sometimes who would ride his bike down to the harbour, the one who had tipped himself and Chris and the twins off to the presence of David's thugs in Diane's house. He shook his head at the memories. It had been a heck of a two weeks.

If you'd asked him, he would have told you life couldn't really change this much, this radically, this fundamentally, in that short a time.

But he wouldn't have believed it, even then. After all, he'd experienced death as a kid when his parents died in an accident. He knew exactly how little time had to do with radical when it came to change.

He knew your whole world could go up in flames, or it could come to a glorious culmination, all in one single instant.

Chris sat down at the table behind Tyler and shoved a brown-betty teapot to one side. "I wish I knew what they're waiting for."

"I don't know either."

"I thought you could all read each other's minds."

"Not really."

"I know."

"Yeah."

Tyler cleared his throat. "Wanna go join Reese? I don't think she'd mind the company."

"I want to give her her space." Chris thought for a moment and changed his answer. "Sure. Fine. Let's go find Reese."

Tyler grabbed his keys from the kitchen counter. "I'll drive."

* * * * *

The way down to the water was tense. As expected, Reese hadn't taken the boat out far. She saw them waving from the dock and came back to pick them up. She'd only taken the skiff, no big deal to turn around and come into the harbour. She handed Chris the anchor rope as they came in, and their hands touched. She blushed. He scowled.

 Rachel Starr Thomson

Man, Tyler thought, but said nothing. His attention was diverted by a kid running down the dock opposite, straight at the water like he never meant to slow down. He looked familiar . . .

He was familiar. It was the kid April was always watching. Nick.

"Hey kid!" The words weren't out of Tyler's mouth before Nick threw himself whole-body off the end of the dock and hit the water with a loud splash, then started swimming like he did not intend to stop. Ever.

There wasn't much boat traffic at this time of day, and the water was calm and not too deep—it was perfectly safe. But the harbour wasn't exactly a normal place to go swimming. What was wrong with the beach?

Nothing.

But there was plenty wrong with the kid.

"Something's wrong," Reese said at the exact moment Tyler knew it was true. The boy was swimming toward the open bay like his arms and legs would never stop churning the water, and Tyler saw himself after his parents died, and Reese after she jumped, and April being April—April with her own past full of things she had just wanted to run away from. And he wanted to jump in after the kid and grab him, and bring him back to the dock and embrace him wet and dripping and shivering and tell him it would all be okay. They were here, and it was going to be okay. He wanted to pick him up in the arms that were Oneness, his arms, and all the family and web he represented now, and never let go.

Instead he just stood on the dock and watched the kid swim, stricken. He didn't know what to do.

He felt Reese next to him like the presence of the sun's warmth on his skin. Thoughts in unison, not shared, but kin. Before he had been Joined, become One, he had wondered if his identity would be swallowed up in the Oneness and he would lose himself. That, he was slowly realizing, was the great fear—the reason people resisted. But Oneness was not a loss of identity. It was not even a loss of separateness. It was the kind of joining that love accomplishes, where each is made his own apex, the best of what he could possibly be, and in that strength chooses to cleave to others because he recognizes that life is not worth living alone.

Tyler had, in fact, felt more than once in the last two weeks that he was only now beginning to understand who he really was and where he was going. What the seed inside Tyler MacKenzie had been containing all these years, ready to sprout and grow into something he did not recognize but had always been meant for.

Watching an eleven-year-old boy swim away from hell, Tyler wondered what seed was in his soul and what it would take to start the process of growth he had been born for.

And Chris. Whether and if Chris would ever embrace this truth that there was more to himself that he was denying, a life he was not supposed to miss.

That had been a surprise too. When Reese first betrayed the existence of the Oneness and Diane first began to explain it to them, Tyler had assumed they were a special class of human beings, as different from normal people as dogs were different from cats. He saw it differently now. Now he was pretty sure everyone was meant to be Oneness. Everyone had that seed. But some chose never to let the seed germinate, and spent their

     Rachel Starr Thomson

whole lives bound up in a hard shell and a dark place, refusing ever to stretch and grow into the sun.

At least, he thought it worked something like that. He was no guru. Just a kid who had gotten swept up in something big, and wished everyone else would do the same thing. And belonged to a Oneness cell and sometimes talked to dead people.

He quirked a smile. You had to hand it to Chris—he might not be ready to join the Oneness himself, but he had put up with a whole lot of weirdness without balking. For love of Tyler, Tyler knew, and for a tentative, slowly growing love of Reese.

Reese was watching Nick, the boy, with a frown. "Do you think we should go after him?"

Tyler took in the spray Nick's arms and legs were kicking up. "I don't think I have that much energy."

"I do," Chris cut in. "You want me to go get him?"

"No," Tyler said, "I don't think so. He'll be okay. He's just working something out."

Reese watched him a few more minutes. He had stopped swimming like a maniac and was floating on his back, staring up into the sky at a flock of gulls circling overhead.

"Yeah, I think you're right," she said.

"It's not easy, being eleven," Tyler said.

"Especially not some kinds of eleven," Chris finished.

The threesome stood and watched him for a while, Reese still standing in the skiff with it rocking gently beneath her, Chris and Tyler on the dock. Nick was just a kid, and none of them really knew him, and yet the harbour at that moment was orbiting around the pull of his personality and his need.

"I'm going to get him," Reese announced after a minute more. But the anchor rope stayed tied, and neither of the boys moved to help.

She stayed put.

* * * * *

On the outskirts of town, a car pulled up to a nondescript gas station, a privately owned affair with a white gull on the sign.

The man who got out was a stranger to the fishing village. He was tall and stood straight with impeccable posture and neatly groomed hair of no particular colour. His wife sat in the car with their two children in the backseat, a boy and a girl about eleven and twelve years old. The wife looked harried. The children were calm.

"Hurry up," the woman called out the window.

He ignored her. Gas would pump at the speed gas would pump. And their reasons for coming to town would wait until they got around to them.

On the front seat next to the wife, a plastic-bound paperback entitled Child Psychology and the Effects of Violence in the Home lay neatly positioned as though it were a centrepiece in the car. Meant to be seen and noted.

In the backseat one of the children, the boy, inched up to ask his mother a question and caught sight of the book. He looked at it with disdain and thought better of asking, settling back into his seat and staring out the window instead.

The girl broke the silence. "Do we have to take him home?"

"We've been over this already," the mother said, testy.

"I already don't like him. He lives here with a bunch of fish. I'll bet he smells," the boy said.

"That's enough."

The father reentered the car, and silence fell. No one challenged his purpose as he hit the accelerator and drove smoothly on toward the village.

* * * * *

April saw the car enter the village streets from her perch on the roof. She'd fallen asleep up there, dozing in the sun with Mary checking on her worriedly every now and again. She wasn't really sure what woke her. But there it was, a long sedan that almost looked like it belonged to an earlier era, like a sleek money car from the '60s, purring into town and reeking of not belonging there. The fishing village didn't care much what era it belonged to; it was a little world of its own. April liked that about it. But this car didn't feel right.

Rubbing sleep from her eyes, she watched it turn and disappear down the hill, motoring off to the east into one of the village's poorer neighbourhoods.

To Nick's house.

Where that insight came from she didn't know. But April had eyes to see. When she knew things, she just knew them. It was a gift—part of what being Oneness meant to her.

She cleared her throat to call out for Mary or Richard and realized they weren't going to hear her from the roof. Gingerly, she picked herself up, keeping the blanket wrapped around her, and walked the flat ledge to the window where she eased herself through. "Mary?" she called. No answer met her ears.

The house, large enough to house a large family comfortably, with four bedrooms upstairs and an extra one down, a big kitchen and a common area designed for meetings and time together, was mostly empty. The Oneness cell in the village was tiny. For years it had been just Mary and Richard, then April. Diane had never lived with them. Even now, she confessed her Oneness only grudgingly. Reese was the newcomer—the one who had brought Diane back into the fold. And Tyler was only newly One. He chose to stay with Chris in their little cottage up on the cliff, overlooking the bay and their history together. No one questioned that it was the right place for him to be.

All of which was why, even though the cell had nearly doubled, the house was still so empty.

"Mary?" No answer again. April poked through the rooms on the ground floor, looking for either of her housemates, but they were gone. Reese, she thought, was out with the boys.

Vaguely guilty because she knew Mary had only stepped out for a few minutes—the cell leader had kept herself within calling distance of April at all times since bringing her home from the killing cave—April pulled a hoodie over her usual tank top and track pants and headed out the door. Nick's neighbourhood was a relatively short walk—only about a mile. And it was a beautiful day. She could make it.

What exactly she was planning to do when she got there, she had no idea. But something about that car had been . . . wrong.

April smelled demons. Danged if she was going to let a little boy deal with them alone.

She didn't think to leave a note.

Nick was in a bad mood. The dive into the harbour hadn't really helped, which made him even more unhappy. Usually water, salt, sun could wash away life for at least a few minutes. Not today. Nothing could wash away the sounds of his parents fighting, the things they said to each other, the way his dad reeked. Nothing could wash away the fear he felt when he saw some of his father's friends hanging around or the anger at his mother for not doing more to protect him.

He'd had the crazy idea that he should talk to the three people on the dock who watched him swim. He'd encountered two of them before, helped them out. And they reminded him of April. Who, somehow, he knew he could trust.

But he hadn't. He'd ignored them.

He scuffed his feet as they carried him home, like he was mad at them for going there. When he'd left home he had wanted to stay out all day. Planned to. Unfortunately, he got hungry. There wasn't usually much to eat at home, but there was even less on the streets.

He reached home and found a car sitting in his driveway. His steps slowed even more. Why was someone here? Today, of all days?

Two kids were in the car. They glared at him. He wanted to glare back, to stake his claim to superiority—this was his house—but he couldn't.

Whoever had driven was inside the house.

He took a tentative step forward just to break the freeze of fear that had come over him.

A hand on his shoulder stopped him.

He looked up. A concerned, pretty face looked back down. She looked worn and sick, with big dark circles under her eyes and lines around her mouth that he didn't think had been there before. It had been weeks since he'd seen her last.

"Stay put for a minute," April told him.

She looked away from him, her hand still firmly on his shoulder, and took in the sight of the children in the backseat. She frowned.

The little girl stuck out her tongue. April just frowned again, and Nick wondered exactly what she was seeing.

They stood together in the driveway. The windows on the house were open, and through the ripped screen, Nick could hear his mother talking to someone. Dad was most likely out drinking. That was where he usually went after a morning like the morning this one had been—after a screaming fight he rarely stuck around. Maybe he would be gone for a few days, even. There was a man's voice in the house now, talking to his mother low and calm. And a woman's voice chiming in.

April seemed to have joined Nick in his freeze. She just stood there with her hand on his shoulder, ignoring those kids and listening to the voices that couldn't be made out properly.

Then, "Hey," she said, "come with me."

"What?"

"Just come with me. We'll get lunch or something. Come on."

She was keeping her voice unnaturally quiet, like she didn't want the grown-ups inside to hear. Nick realized he didn't think of April as a grown-up. She was a kid, like him, only one who could be trusted to have good ideas and help him keep out of his parents' way.

But it seemed a little insane to just leave. He was pretty sure the people inside the house had something to do with him. Otherwise, why was he so afraid? So it would be a good idea to stay here and find out what.

The pressure on his shoulder turned into a pull. "Let's go. Right now. What do you want, a hamburger?"

"Fish and chips," he said. The words just came out of his mouth.

"Okay," she said. "Fish and chips. Come on."

"They'll see," Nick said, not pointing at the kids in the car but meaning them.

April understood. "It's okay. Let's just go. They won't know where we're going."

They turned on their heels, like one person, and headed away from the house, back up toward the heart of the village. Nick figured they were going to the pub. It was the best place to get fish and chips in the afternoon, and they would let him in because it wasn't evening hours yet. He wondered if Dad was there. Not that he would notice Nick if he was.

At first it seemed like that was where they were going. Then April took a sudden hard right and charged up the road toward the neighbourhood overlooking the slope. This wasn't the way to the pub.

"Hey," Nick said, "I want fish and chips." He didn't, really . . . he just wanted some control of this situation.

"You'll get them," April said. She sounded strained. "I just . . . I need to sit down first. Just come with me?"

This, Nick knew, was stupid. April was technically a stranger, even though she sometimes spent time with him. He didn't actually know anything about her. You weren't supposed to "just go" with strangers anywhere, especially not to their homes. He only justified going to the pub with her because it wasn't exactly like his home was so much safer. So he stopped.

The reality of the situation must have hit her too, because she stopped and crouched down to eye level with him. She brushed a lock of wispy blonde hair out of her eye. Nick was struck by the strange mix of frail and tough that was April. The blonde hair and the weary expression and the black rose tattoo on her shoulder, which he knew was under the hoodie because she usually just wore a tank. She was strange and very interesting, which was half the reason he'd let her become a sort of friend in the first place.

The other half was that he just really needed a friend sometimes, and he didn't have any other options.

"Listen," she said, "I know this isn't really kosher. But I need

    Rachel Starr Thomson

you to come back to my house with me. I was going to take you to the pub, but it's . . . I don't think it's safe right now. Nick, I promise I won't hurt you. I promise I'm safe."

He looked her in the eyes and knew she was telling the truth. "I'm not allowed to go to strangers' houses," he said.

Why did he even say that? It sounded stupid coming out of his mouth.

But to his surprise, April nodded. "Okay. Okay, I get that." She bit her lip. "There's a boat on the harbour. A little skiff. Friends of mine own it. Will you go there for a little while? Just sit there and wait for me?"

"I was down there before," he told her. "Your friends were there."

"Good!" Her face lit up. "You can go hang out around them. Don't get in the boat if you don't want to. Just stay where they can see you. Can you do that?"

He looked at her cock-eyed. "What are you going to do?"

"Talk to your mother," April said, squaring her shoulders like she had just said something very courageous. "I need you to come home with me, Nick, because I need to keep an eye on you. Something is going on. I think you're in danger. So I'm going to talk to your mother and get her permission, so you'll know it's safe to come with me. Okay?"

Nick considered it. The whole situation was cockeyed and he knew it. His mother, he knew from long experience, was not safe or good at keeping him safe. April, in his experience, was a great deal more trustworthy. And yet he knew there was something very right about April going to his mother for permission to keep him safe, about her asking to be known as officially okay.

But when he thought about April going back to the house, with that car still in the driveway, he felt scared again.

His voice came out sounding small. "I don't want you to go back there right now."

He hadn't forgotten the last time April tried to help him. He had no idea what had happened to her after the men knocked her out and dragged her away—she struck him now as something of a cat with nine lives—but he didn't want it to happen again.

With one question, they had switched roles, and Nick would do anything he could to keep her safe.

"I'll go home with you," he said. "It will be okay. Mum won't mind."

She won't even notice, an inner voice told him.

Unless those people in the car are looking for me, he answered back.

Which they were. He just knew they were.

But April had set her eyes back toward Nick's house, and it was clear she wasn't going to give up her new plan that easily.

"No, this is right," she said. She set her eyes back on Nick like she had just remembered him. "You should go—to the dock."

Memories of the thugs attacking April had turned him off that idea. "I don't want to go down there."

"Then just go to my house. It really will be okay. I'll tell you how to get there. Mary—I live with her—will take care of you. Tell her you want lunch. Fish and chips. I'll come soon."

"What are you going to do?" he asked, his voice quavering. He wanted to sound manly but couldn't.

     Rachel Starr Thomson

"I'm going to talk to your mother," April said.

Nick felt that a man ought to be able to set his own course in life, and that his day or his destiny shouldn't rest on a conversation between two women, even if one of them had birthed him. But he was acutely conscious that he was not a man yet, and that April was braver and better than he was. Because whatever was back at his house, it terrified him more the farther away he got from it—like somehow the steps he'd put between them were clearing a fog and allowing him to see clearly a monster he had not imagined as nearly frightening enough. He grabbed her hand like a toddler and held it tightly.

"Please don't. Please don't go."

She crouched again and regarded him gently, not without a little fear in her own eyes. "What are you afraid of?"

"I don't know. Please don't go."

But firmly, gently, like a mother herself though Nick was sure she did not have children, she pressed her hand on his shoulder and said, "Get on up to the house. It's the one at the top of the slope there—with the grey shingled roof. The big house. You see it?" He nodded. "I'll be coming as soon as I've talked to your mum. It's going to be fine, Nick. There are some things I need to know."

He swallowed hard and released her hand when she withdrew.

He didn't know what else to do.

* * * * *

April slowed down just a fraction as she approached Nick's

house again. The car was still in the driveway but was clearly on its way out—a woman was sitting in the front passenger seat, and the kids were squirming impatiently in a way that indicated they expected to leave now. The driver's seat was still empty.

So he was still in the house.

April cleared her throat and squared her shoulders and forced herself to pick up her pace all the way to the front door, like she was supposed to be there. The voices, a man and Nick's mother, came through more clearly now.

"We'll be back this evening," the man was saying.

"I'm sorry about this," the mother said, fretting. "He just takes off, and I don't know where he goes. If—"

"There's no need to apologize," the man said, in a voice so soothing it sent shivers down April's spine. "We understand."

We. April knocked before the man could say another word.

"Oh, who the—I am sorry about this."

"Not at all."

The door swung open. Nick's mother stood there. She looked much like April had expected: like a young woman harried into old age too fast. Her hair was styled and her lipstick was too red, but her clothes were tatty and her eyes said life was hard, far too hard.

She was sober. April wasn't sure if she had expected that.

"Hi," April said. Not her most brilliant opening speech ever.

"Can I help you?" The tone was not exactly friendly, yet there was—welcome?—in it. Or beseeching? She was relieved, April realized, relieved to not be talking to the man in the living

    Rachel Starr Thomson

room anymore.

"Yes," April said, trying to put words together even as her eyes strayed past the woman to the cluttered, dirty entranceway and past that to the living room where the man stood. Tall and impeccably dressed and impeccably coiffed. Imposing and commanding.

And possessed.

She was sure of it.

"Yes," she said, her voice gaining a little more force. "I want to talk to you about Nick."

"About—"

"Nick, your son."

"I know my own son's name." The woman sounded resentful.

"I know—I'm sorry." April forced her eyes away from the man and his demonic aura and made herself focus on Nick's mother. "I'm . . . I'm April."

She paused, and it took the woman a moment. "Shelley," she finally said. "Look, I don't know why you're here, but . . ."

"Please, don't let me impose," April interrupted. She stepped aside. The man had come out of the living room and was standing in the entranceway. "You were just leaving?" she said.

"Yes," he answered, looking at her with a slow, measured gaze.

Yes, I am, her spirit said. I am what you think. I am Oneness. And I see you. You are not unknown or unhindered here. Take that message back to wherever you've come from.

She hoped her posture, her eyes, conveyed some of that.

The man elbowed past her—she made enough room for him to get by, but not enough room for him to feel entirely comfortable doing it—and said good-bye to Shelley.

"We'll be back," he said.

"Yes, I understand," she told him. "I'm sorry, again."

"There's no need." The man's eyes were fixed on April, and Shelley seemed to be growing antsy at the subverbal interaction that was clearly occurring on her doorstep. "He's sure to be here one of these times. Soon." Her tone betrayed guilt, and something worse—fear. From the man, an unmistakable aura of threat flowed.

Shelley said something else, something April didn't catch, and in a minute the car was purring out of the driveway back to wherever it had come. The children turned themselves around in the seat and glared at April the whole time it took for the car to pass out of sight.

"Well," April said. "May I come in?"

With an expression somewhere between annoyed and relieved, Shelley stepped aside and invited April into the shabby living room. April pointedly ignored her surroundings—it was the sort of liquor-stained, hurt-driven place that would drag up way too many of her own memories if she focused on it. Instead, she looked Shelley in the eye.

The woman dodged her gaze. She leaned back against the ratted couch and said, "What about Nick?"

April realized that she didn't actually know what she was going to say. In the pause while she tried to figure out an answer, Shelley charged on.

"I do my best, I do—he's getting so angry, but I don't want

     Rachel Starr Thomson

him to ruin his life like us." Her eyes filled with tears. "He's my kid. I love him. "

April faltered forward, aware that she was treading on unexpectedly sacred ground.

"What do you think he needs most?"

"I guess he was right," Shelley answered, wiping her nose on her sleeve and sniffling. "He needs more security, a routine . . . a normal family life."

"Who was right?" April interrupted. "The man who was just here?"

"Yes," Shelley answered, sniffling again. "He's some kinda child shrink. He wants to take Nick to a children's home in Lincoln."

"You don't want to send him," April said. Flat statement. No question.

Shelley looked up, surprised. "It's best for him . . . I want to do what's best for N—"

"But you're his mother, and that man scares you."

Shelley was silent. This time, her eyes met April's. The expression there shook April more than she had expected it to.

She wondered if her own mother had ever looked like that, and April had been too hurt-blind to see it. The look was love. Harried, exhausted, resourceless love. But real all the same.

"Yeah," Shelley said. "Yeah, he does."

April formed her words slowly. "I can't tell you why, but you're right to be scared. That man . . . going with him wouldn't be better for Nick."

Shelley burst into tears. "But he was right! This place isn't good for Nick. We ain't good for Nick. His dad is always drinking and slapping him around. He said—that man—he said they were going to come and arrest us and take Nick away if we wouldn't do the right thing. He said—"

"I'll take him," April said.

Somewhere in the last moment she had moved across the room, and now her arms were around Shelley. The woman's tears turned into sobs, and she shook in April's hold. "It's bad for him," she kept saying. "We're bad for him. But I don't wanna send him away."

April just held her for a long time and let her cry. The tears were good. Finally she said, "He can come with me. I'll take him."

This time Shelley really seemed to hear her. She pulled back and wiped away her tears. April kept going. "I don't live far away. We're in a good home . . . there are a few of us. You can meet us all. We'll take care of him. We'll keep him safe. I promise."

Shelley's face was red and ragged from crying, but she nodded.

"And we'll keep that man away from him," April finished. "Promise. No one is going to come after you."

Shelley stood, pushing April away a little, and disappeared into the kitchen. She reappeared a few minutes later slightly less bedraggled, and offered April a glass of water.

"No, thank you," April said.

"You ain't like other people," Shelley said flatly. "Neither was he—that man. But you're different again."

April nodded. "It's true. Do I scare you?"

"No." Shelley eyed her up and down, as though trying to figure out exactly what she was. "You're from God."

April smiled, a small smile. "It's true. We are. I am."

Shelley nodded. This time the gesture was final. "Then Nick will be fine with you. He likes you, anyway . . . I know you pick him up sometimes when he runs off and take him for lunch. I should say thanks for that."

"It's my privilege," April said.

"You know about Nick, don't you? The kind of kid he is and the kind of life he's had?"

"Yes," April told her. "I was that kind of kid. I had this kind of life." She hesitated. "He's not the only one who can get out, you know. You too—we can help you."

Shelley waved her hand and smiled warily. "You're helping just by getting that kid out of our hair."

The words sounded a little uncaring. But April knew what she meant.

* * * * *

When April arrived home, Nick was sitting at the dining room table ploughing his way through a mountain of golden fish and chips. With a sea of tartar sauce on the side, and a Coke. In a frosted glass.

Mary shot April a look as she came in the door, and April just laughed.

"See?" she asked, nudging Nick in the shoulder. "I told you she would feed you."

Nick looked up at her and raised his Coke like a beer stein. "Thanks," he said.

"So when does this get explained?" Mary asked, clearly wanting the eleven-year-old in on the discussion. Best if they were all on the same page from the start.

"Well," April said, "he needed lunch. And it turns out, he could use a quiet place to live. I talked to his mum just now. She said he can stay with us."

The look on Mary's face clearly said, There is more to this story, and I want to hear it. But out loud she just responded, "Ah. Well, there's plenty of room. He can have his pick upstairs."

"There's a room that looks out over the slope," April told him. "You can see all the way down to the harbour."

"Is that how you always knew when I was biking or running down there?" Nick asked.

"Very clever. No. I sit on the roof. But that room is how I get out."

"Gracious, don't give him ideas!" Mary burst out. "It's bad enough trying to make sure you don't fall and break your neck."

"That has never even almost ever happened," April rejoined.

Nick was eyeing them both suspiciously, as though he wasn't sure what to make of the happy back-and-forth between them. The Coke, however, held him off from becoming too suspicious. April stuck her head in the fridge and reached for one for herself.

Mary cut her off by edging her small frame into the door and relocating the Coke seconds before April could reach it. She glared. "No."

"But I'm recovering . . ." April managed weakly.

          Rachel Starr Thomson

"Emphasis on the 'ing.' You can drink that poison again when you're able to handle it."

April pointed at Nick. "How come he gets poison?"

Mary smiled, and the love in her eyes made them crinkle deeply. She wasn't an old woman by any means—just into her early fifties, and fit and young for her age—but in love she was old, and in grief, and in other things that deepened a life and made it more than its years. "Because he's charming," she said.

Nick didn't laugh. He was still looking at April and Mary like they had grown a third head between them. But there was something in his eyes, somewhere between fear and discovery, that April knew would grow into a laugh given time.

She intended to give it lots of time.

"Enjoy your poison," she told Nick, passing out of the kitchen. "I'll be back to tell you what your mom said."

On her way up the stairs, April felt a wave of exhaustion blast into her, and she faltered. Mary was right, of course—she wasn't well yet. It took some time to recover from being dehydrated and starved and hit over the head and nearly killed.

She turned left at the top of the stairs and eased into her room, dropping onto her bed with a heavy sigh. A sketchbook sat on the bedside table. She gave herself a minute to pull up some energy and then reached for the book and flipped it open.

The sketchbook opened automatically to the page she wanted, and Nick's face looked up at her, sketched in charcoal with so much detail that April had sometimes been tempted to talk to it in an attempt to change the sad, resentful expression in its lines.

The sketch wasn't original. She had drawn the first one on the wall of the cave where she was starving to death, accompanied by a woman who had died several hundred years before and who had confirmed April's belief that Nick was something special, something to be rescued, and something particularly connected to her. His face was just one of many sketches that had come to her there, some known to her and some not, telling stories and forthtelling prophecy all over the walls of the cave. She had done the work in mud, clay, and rock. She had known herself to be not the original artist: like stone or a paintbrush in her own hand, she was an instrument in the hand of the Spirit, and it was the Spirit who imaged through her.

It was not common that the Spirit would work so clearly, so pointedly. So Nick's prominence in the cave art gave her to know that he was important. His too-serious eyes had looked down on her all while she lay dying, and now those same eyes were sitting at the dining room table, peering through a frosted glass at a tall Coke and watching Mary warily, with fear and with hope. And April did not feel ready, or equipped, or like she knew at all what she was doing. She had faced off with another power at the house: she had challenged the demons that were coming for Nick. She had exposed herself and revealed her care for the boy. She knew that would lead to something, too—that it was enormously unlikely the dark powers would just back off.

So now she was at war, and she didn't know what to do next.

That was why she had come upstairs. She needed a moment to collect her thoughts and tap into the power that was still painting, still storytelling, all through her life and the lives of the Oneness.

With the sketches still open in her lap, she closed her eyes and breathed, "Come and help me."

And she knew she was heard.

 Rachel Starr Thomson

That evening Tyler went to the cell house. No one called or put out a flare, but he knew he was wanted. They all did. When he arrived, even Diane was there—excusing her presence by saying she'd come to check on April, but there for the same reason they all were: to meet Nick and to strengthen each other. Richard came home from work and led them all in prayer, which was a kind of cracking the heavens Tyler could never have prepared himself for, and absolutely nothing like the "Now I lay me down to sleep" sort of recitation most people thought of when they heard the word. When the Oneness prayed, they pulled back curtains and charged into the reality that was Spirit. After the fact, Tyler had no idea what they had prayed "about." That wasn't really how prayer worked. It was a ride, not a meeting.

He got back to the cottage around nine. Chris met him at the door.

"I'm going to Lincoln tomorrow," Chris announced. "You want to come?"

Tyler eyed his friend suspiciously. His whole body was still tingling with the rush of prayer, and everything in him felt like it was standing at attention. Chris's words, in contrast to how innocuous they sounded, were portentous.

"Why?" Tyler asked.

Chris shrugged. "I want to get a few things for the boats."

"And?"

Chris's brown eyes sparkled. "You may have to wait until Richard says go. I don't."

Tyler shook his head. "You can't just wade into a fight with demons, Chris. You know that. You can't even fight them."

"I don't intend to fight. Just to learn."

Tyler pushed past his friend and threw his coat on the kitchen table. "I don't know what you think you're going to accomplish."

"I have no plans," Chris said. "I just want to show up and see what the universe does."

"The universe?"

"It's a big place, they tell me. Unpredictable. Full of angels and demons and people like you."

Tyler sat down and leaned his head in his hands, scrubbing his face. "This is a bad idea, Chris."

Chris sat down across the table and stared until Tyler was forced to look up and meet his gaze.

"Why did you join the Oneness?" he asked.

The question caught Tyler off guard. "It . . . I just had to.

     Rachel Starr Thomson

It was meant to be."

"And I have to go into Lincoln tomorrow. You're not the only one fate has in its grip."

"It's not exactly fate."

"I'm not exactly into philosophy. Tyler, something in that city has attacked and hurt people I love. That something is still out there, still growing, and still plotting. I can't just sit here and let things be. If nothing else, I need to know more about what's going on."

Tyler thought it over. "Fine."

"So are you coming?"

He hesitated another second or two. "Yes."

Chris smiled grimly. "Good."

"That kid is at the cell house," Tyler said. In the confrontation with Chris's plans, he had almost forgotten.

His friend looked surprised. "What?"

"April went and got him," Tyler said.

"What, like kidnapped him? You can't just . . ."

"She talked to his mother. It looks like he's going to be living at the cell house for a while."

Chris stood. "Interesting. I'm glad."

"Me too. Chris . . ." Tyler hesitated, but decided to charge on. It wasn't like Chris wasn't already deeper into the Oneness's business than most people would ever get. "She said she encountered a demon at Nick's house. Some man who was there trying to convince his mother to send Nick away with him. To a children's home in Lincoln."

Something flared in Chris's eyes. "Oh yeah? Does she know the name of the place?"

Tyler shook his head. "She stood off the demon and then talked the mother into sending Nick to the cell house instead. Said it wasn't too hard—the woman was scared, even though she didn't know why."

Chris punched his palm. "Plan to be out most of the day tomorrow," he said. "I've just added a few more places to our list to visit."

He didn't have to say. They'd be looking up children's homes. It wasn't much to go on, but Chris was so punchy, he'd track any sign of demons into their own dens. Tyler hadn't been long around the Oneness and their multidimensional kind of life, but even he knew Chris's determination to get involved, to find the hive and force some kind of confrontation, was lunacy.

But it wasn't lunacy he could oppose. He knew why Chris did it. Chris lived, breathed, moved to protect and care for those he loved. Chief among those were his mother, Tyler, and Reese. Their involvement with the Oneness put them all at risk, all the time, and Chris knew it. So he wasn't going to rest while an obvious, aggressive, centralized threat was out there, undealt with. Chris was an army all his own, determined to stamp out dissidents before they could start something that would take his whole country down in flames.

So. They would go in the morning.

"How are you planning to find them?" Tyler asked. "Them" was intentionally broad. Demons, people under the influence of, children's homes. Whatever.

"We've got a few leads," Chris said. "We'll follow them. You

 Rachel Starr Thomson

should go to bed. Get a good night's sleep."

"Is Reese coming with us?"

Chris shot him a look. "Of course not."

"She can handle herself pretty good," Tyler said defensively.

"She'll have to. But not yet. And I'm not taking her back there unless I have to."

Tyler felt a shot of fear go down his back. "There" could only mean one place, and he didn't want to go.

The warehouse.

*　*　*　*　*

When morning broke over the bay, the light coming over the cliffs from the east and spreading itself out across the water, it broke in golden perfection. The air was warm, summer beautiful, and the cliffs were sandy yellow in its glow. The water was deep blue; the pines and scrub on the mountainsides green with life lush and growing. Tyler stood on the front step of the cottage and just breathed it all in, thankful.

Behind him, Chris was starting the truck. It wasn't yet six-thirty in the morning, but he wanted to be on the road as soon as possible. They would grab breakfast on the way. The city was a good hour's drive inland, and Chris wanted to get the jump on—well, whatever they were going to find.

Tyler stayed outside, gazing over the water, as Chris revved the engine in the carport. The cottage behind him was a little shabby at first glance, but that was only age and the effects of salt and wind. Chris had always kept it up, and in reality it was tight and neatly managed, a sturdy little bulwark against anything that could come up to challenge it, be it wind or high weather or death or change.

They certainly had weathered plenty of the latter. All things considered, it seemed appropriate that Tyler had chosen to keep living here after he Joined. The cell house was open to him always, and they would have loved for him to come—and part of him wanted to, wanted to bask in the connection of Oneness all the time. But his life had been with Chris a long time. And as Chris had not abandoned him, Tyler saw no real reason to leave.

Chris drove the truck out of the carport and honked the horn. Tyler pulled his eyes away from the bay. Time to go.

They pulled into Lincoln less than an hour later; traffic between the city and the fishing village was light, and they'd gotten on the road before the onslaught of work-related traffic could hit. Chris had a city map on the front seat between them, along with a giant telephone book that serviced most of the county.

But the first stop, they didn't need to look up an address. Tyler was surprised, but he said nothing.

The Lincoln cell. David's old home base.

Tyler felt the familiar pull of Oneness as they pulled onto the quiet, slightly rundown block where the house was located. The beat of hearts in tune with his, the sense of immense comfort, belonging, supercharged strength as the talents and gifts of many came together in one. The cell here was far bigger than the one in the village; at any given time there might be close to twenty people living in the house. An old triplex had been converted for the purpose. Tyler had no idea what people in the

     Rachel Starr Thomson

neighbourhood thought about the cell. Maybe they figured it was a student home. Or a cult.

This cell was also far more active than the one in the village. Reese had become Joined here and had done her apprenticeship in spiritual warfare in this place: based in the city, the cell was regularly exposed to far more demonic activity than hit the quiet little bay town where Mary and Richard had held their post for so many years. Reese was a fighter, an experienced undercover warrior in a battle zone most people didn't know existed.

But the cell lay at the heart of the war in another, more frightening way as well. Their leader of many years, David, had turned against the Oneness—and somehow, they hadn't known. He had joined forces with the enemy, nearly destroyed Reese, almost undone the work of the Oneness throughout the city and further. He had fathered a hive. April's paintings had exposed him.

Where he was now was anyone's guess.

The cell was still just trying to pick up the pieces.

Chris parked on the street across from the house and jumped out into tufty, scratchy grass on the edge of the curb. No one around here made landscaping a priority. The cell house was by far the best kept on the block. Tyler eased his way out of the car a little more slowly. The presence of the Oneness heightened his sensitivity to the whole area, and the whole area, to him, felt bruised. Purple and swollen and maybe still bleeding on the inside.

The front screen door swung open with a creak and a bang, and a girl about nineteen threw herself out. Long, thick dark hair streamed out behind her. She wore a T-shirt and cutoff shorts and did not look a thing like the ruthless swordswoman

Tyler and Chris both knew her to be.

"Good morning!" Angelica called as she trotted down the sidewalk toward them. "Come in! Coffee's on."

She looked at Tyler and their eyes caught, and in that split second exchanged the pain of David's betrayal. The Oneness did not fracture without everyone feeling it. The more members present, the more compounded the pain.

"Thanks," Chris said, ignoring—or not feeling—the undercurrents. By the time they reached Angelica and all headed for the door, her twin, Tony, had appeared, along with two or three other younger faces.

Tony swung the door open and stepped aside, holding it for their guests. He looked considerably less awake than his twin sister, but just as glad to see them.

The common room in the Lincoln house was large, easily big enough to serve as a small hall, and arranged for visiting with several different sets of couches, chairs, and coffee tables grouped together a convenient distance from each other. Cell members were sprawled out across the various configurations, eating breakfast, drinking coffee, reading, or talking quietly. It looked like a college dorm, little indication that these were warriors, servants of God, labourers alongside the angels. Tyler drank in the sense of community and let it fill him, even in its hurt and brokenness. For a moment it was almost overwhelming. Added to it was the sense of expansion he sometimes felt at odd moments—a sense of the reach, of the immensity of the Oneness, that extended far beyond this house or this room, crossing time and space and even the boundaries of mortality. He half-expected to see one of the Cloud, those members of the Oneness who had crossed over the River Styx but maintained

          Rachel Starr Thomson

their connection, keeping ghostly vigil and casting envious glances at the coffee. There was no one—that he could see.

Tony led them to a little huddle of padded chairs. Chris didn't sit. Tyler did, for a moment, and then shifted back to his feet. Last time they were here, meeting like this, it was David hosting them, sitting them down, giving them information. Telling them lies about Reese. No wonder this place felt so battered. David had influenced every corner of this house and every person who lived in it. His absence was tangible. His betrayal even more so.

"How's Reese?" Tony asked. He was sitting, ignoring the fact that no one else was. Angelica hovered behind his chair.

"Recovering," Chris said. "Happy in the village."

"And April?"

Tyler smiled. "Back on her feet and adopting village kids."

Tony arced an eyebrow. "Oh yeah?"

"That's actually why we're here," Chris cut in. "The kid was in April's cave paintings. And he's got demons after him. Our fight isn't over."

Tony and Angelica exchanged a glance. "We knew that."

Chris blew out a frustrated breath. "Then I hope to God you're doing more about it than the village is."

"We're watching," Tony said slowly. "I don't like it, but it's all gone pretty undercover since the fight at the warehouse."

"What's still happening there?" Chris pushed.

"Nothing," Angelica answered. "They've vacated. We don't know where the hive is based now. If the core has regrouped, we don't know where it is."

Chris slammed the edge of a chair he was standing beside. "Blast."

Tony shrugged apologetically. He was still seated, impressing Tyler with his ability to remain completely unintimidated by Chris. "We're keeping our eyes open. When they resurface, we'll find them."

"You don't know where they are at all?" Chris pressed. "No signs of activity?"

"Nothing. We know there's a hive . . . somewhere. But it's not showing itself."

"Well, maybe we have a place for you to start looking," Chris said. "You know anything about children's homes in the area?"

Another exchanged glance. "No," Angelica said.

"The demon that came after this kid—Nick—it came in the head of a children's home. Or at least that's what he said he was. Tried to take the kid away, but April got to his mother and convinced her to let the cell take care of him for now."

Tony whistled. "And the demon knows it?"

"April confronted it. Sort of," Tyler said. "She's pretty sure it knows about her, anyway."

"So much for Reese resting up in a quiet village."

"There's not much action happening yet," Chris said, defensive. "But I figure what does happen will start here. Can't we find it and choke it off before it gets to the village?"

"Maybe," Angelica said slowly. "But if it's a hive, it's not always that easy."

"Why not?" Chris said. "You two are fighters. Just go in

    Rachel Starr Thomson

there and slay the dragon."

"A hive is people, Chris," Tony said. "We can't go in and slay people."

"Well, what do you do with them then?"

"Take care of them," Angelica said. "Help them. Try to set them free."

Chris made a quietly frustrated noise, but he didn't argue. "So that's it?" he finally said. "You can't tell us anything because you don't know where the hive is or what it's doing."

"That's about it, yes," Tony said. "We're sorry, Chris. We do have our eyes open."

"Yeah," Chris said. "I guess I just feel like you guys are in a big fight . . . I'd be more proactive."

"We're always in a fight," Angelica said. "Every single day. A lot of it is waiting."

On the way out to the car a few minutes later, Tyler said quietly, "They're wounded, too."

"What?"

"I know you're frustrated, and I get why, but they aren't just in a fight—they're hurt. They need time to recover. Like Reese."

"None of them are broken like Reese was," Chris argued.

"They lost David. That isn't a small thing."

The sun was starting to burn hot, even though it was just past eight, and the air held the heaviness of gathering humidity. Chris trudged to the truck with a frown and pulled the door open. "You feel it too?" he asked.

Tyler winced. "Yeah. I do."

"I forget sometimes."

Tyler smiled. "Good."

"Why?"

"Because it means nothing has really changed. I've still got your back; you've still got mine."

"Everything has changed," Chris said. Then he grinned. "But yeah."

"So where are we going?" Tyler asked as he climbed into the passenger's seat.

"The warehouse."

"They said it's empty."

"I want to see for myself."

Tyler grimaced. "If you insist."

Chris pulled out and drove the truck through an enormous pothole, clunking down over it as they rumbled back out to the main street. "Besides, it'll be fun. Old times sake."

"We almost died in there."

"I'm being sarcastic."

"Uh-huh."

The drive to the warehouse took twenty minutes. It was a classic empty building in an industrial part of town, surrounded by truck lots and more warehouses. The chain-link fence was locked, so they parked on the street outside and jumped over to get into the parking lot outside one of the loading docks.

They stood side by side a moment, looking over the building's unimpressive facade. Hard to believe that last they'd been here, they had been in a pitched battle with forces of evil so real and so repulsive that they seemed like the stuff of the worst old German folk tales . . . the kind of evil only children believed in.

The thought shook Tyler for a moment. He wondered what sort of people believed in him—if he had really become something so out of the ordinary pale of human existence that it took belief in fairies and dragons, or angels and demons, to consider him real and not just a product of delusion.

But the battle that happened here was real—very, very real. They had almost not lived through it.

"Chris," Tyler said quietly, "why are we here?"

"For Reese," he said. And that was all he needed to say.

Last time, too, they had been here for Reese.

Chris started toward the door on the side of the loading dock. Tyler paused a moment to let himself feel the place. The air felt stained, almost inky. But the rank evil that had held court here was gone.

The cell was right. The core had moved on.

The door was unlocked, which Tyler didn't find surprising. He stepped in after Chris. The place was dark, empty except for a couple of pallets loaded with boxes of something. It didn't seem to matter what.

The chill Tyler felt was all in his memory.

Chris wandered off a bit, into the dark. He found a light switch and flipped it, not that it made much difference—a few bare lightbulbs, high up, technically gave light but mostly just showed up how dark and dingy the place was. Tyler hung back by the door.

Hive   47

They left after Chris got tired of wandering through the dark.

When they stepped back out into the sun and the increasingly humid air, Tyler was surprised at how much oppression he could feel lifting off. He hadn't been aware of it when they were inside.

They headed toward the truck, Chris muttering something. Louder, he said, "Well, that was a waste of time."

"They did tell us the core had moved."

Chris stopped and glared. Tyler held up a hand defensively. "They did."

"Sorry," Chris said. "It's not your fault."

Tyler nodded and look forward toward the truck.

"Hey," he said. "Who's that?"

Chris looked up quickly. Someone had ducked behind the truck. Without losing an instant, Chris was jogging toward him. He leaped the fence and broke into a run.

"Hey!" he shouted. "Hey, stop a minute!"

The figure by the truck had tensed as though to run, but he—Tyler could see clearly enough now to make out a teenage boy—opted to stop and wait instead. He was shaking by the time Chris reached him.

Chris stopped short of threatening the teen, backing off into as unintimidating a stance as he could manage while still positioning himself to discourage the kid from bolting. The teen was a stranger—maybe sixteen or seventeen. His eyes ran furtively from side to side.

"Mind telling me what you're doing here?" Chris asked.

     Rachel Starr Thomson

The teen's mouth opened like he was going to answer, but before a word came out, Tyler got within range. The kid's reaction was startling. His eyes open wide, he immediately tried to run. This time Chris blocked him.

"Not yet," Chris said firmly. He had the boy between the truck and a fence, with Tyler just beyond the truck bed. "We want to know what you're doing here. And who you are."

"I'm nobody," the kid stammered. "Honest."

"Well, you're wrong there," Tyler said. "Nobody's nobody."

Chris ignored the comment. "What are you doing here? You want something with my truck? With us?"

"No, no," the kid said, his eyes panicked. "I just . . . wanted to see."

"To see what?"

The kid's eyes flicked to the warehouse. "That place . . . stuff happens there. Freaky stuff. I wanted to see what would happen to you."

This time Tyler caught the way the kid's eyes kept shifting to him. He had angled his back against the fence so he could see both Chris and Tyler, but despite the fact it was Chris who had him backed into a corner and was demanding answers from him, it was definitely Tyler who scared him more. Why? He was about to ask but decided it would be counterproductive. Better to let Chris handle this and hope he would ask the right questions.

"What have you seen happen here?" Chris asked. "And when?"

They were good questions. The kid cast another nervous look at Tyler and shifted his feet.

"It was just . . . just yesterday," the kid said. "Last night. My girlfriend; she's all into this kind of stuff."

"What kind of stuff?" Chris asked.

Now the kid looked suspicious. His eyes narrowed. "If you don't know, why are you here?"

"It's a warehouse," Chris pointed out. "Maybe we came to check out some business."

"You hopped the fence," the kid answered. "You don't belong here any more than I do."

His momentary belligerence vanished when he looked at Tyler again, and he shrank back.

Weird, Tyler thought.

The teen was skinny and average height for his age, his hair dark and greasy, his skin riddled. He wore a black T-shirt with some band's logo and a pair of jeans. He didn't look any more spiritually sensitive than your typical narcissistic high schooler. But he was definitely reacting to something in Tyler.

"Come on," Chris said. "Tell us what kind of stuff goes on here. What's your girlfriend into?"

"Freaky stuff," the kid said. He leaned against the fence and cast a wary glance at Tyler. "They were going to hold a séance or something. You know, try to talk to the dead."

"That's dangerous," Tyler heard himself say, surprised at his own words. After all, he'd spent a fair bit of time recently in the company of dead people. But the Cloud was different—he didn't know much, but he did know that. They weren't exactly ghosts, weren't exactly dead. They were still part of the same Oneness. Séances, attempts to manipulate the natural order of

     Rachel Starr Thomson

things through the occult—that was dangerous.

Figures some group would move into the warehouse and try to do it there. The core was gone, but the kind of spiritual activity they had generated in that building was sure to attract all kinds of crackpots. And people more dangerous than crackpots.

"Your girlfriend part of some group?" Chris asked.

"Why do you want to know?"

"Like you," Chris said. "I'm curious about what goes on here. That's why we're here. We . . . heard some things, about the warehouse, and came to check it out."

"It's just some friends from school," the kid said. "They mess around with, you know, spells and things. My girlfriend's all into solstices and candles and whatever."

"Not you, though?"

The kid shrugged. "It's weird. Interesting, but weird."

"Have they been meeting here for a while?"

"No," the kid said, shaking his head with surprising vehemence. "Not until that creep came along. Now they all do whatever he says. And he says this place is all, I don't know . . . like a spiritual centre or something."

The unmistakable note of jealousy and resentment in the teen's voice told more of the story: whoever "the creep" was, he had way more influence on this kid's girlfriend than he liked. Which probably had something to do with why he was stationed outside the warehouse spying on people who came in.

But which didn't explain his aversion to Tyler.

"Who's 'that creep'?" Chris asked.

The kid shrugged, but the resentment on his face furrowed deeper. "Some college guy. Thinks he's god or something."

"He have a name?"

"Doesn't everybody?"

Chris contained his impatience with admirable self-control. "You know it?"

"No," the kid said. "He just calls himself the Wizard."

Tyler hid a smirk. "The Wizard? What does he think he is, a supervillain?"

"He thinks he's a hero," the kid said.

"Or a god," Chris reiterated.

"That's what I said."

"They meet here regularly?" Chris asked.

"Last night was the first time. But I think they'll come back. Look, I'm not into what they're into, but something happened here last night. They came out all . . . freaky, like I said."

Chris frowned. "Can you explain 'freaky'?"

The kid's eyes shifted to Tyler again, and his body language grew more antsy. "Like him," he blurted.

Tyler felt like he'd been slapped. "What do you mean?"

"Don't ask me, man," the kid said. "You're not normal, that's all I'm saying. Like them."

"Are they still . . . freaky?" Chris asked. "I mean, did it last overnight?"

"I don't know. My girlfriend seems okay. The Wizard is like that all the time."

Chris folded his big arms and stood a little taller. "You know where to find this Wizard guy?"

"No," the kid said. "I don't know where he lives. He hangs out by the school sometimes. But mostly he just seems to get word out and people go to him. Like here."

"Do you know when they'll be back here?"

"No," the kid said. He looked both ways and started to move toward Chris, but his path was still blocked.

"Look," he said, "I told you all I know. You can't just keep me here."

Chris didn't move. "We aren't keeping you. We're just talking. It's important that I find this guy."

"You got a score to settle or something?"

"Kind of."

The kid looked torn. It was clear he didn't want to be in the middle of this, but setting someone as big and imposing—and determined—as Chris on his rival was an attractive idea.

"I can call you," he finally said. "Tell you when they're meeting again."

"How do you know that?" Tyler asked.

"I keep an eye on my girl," the kid said.

Great, Tyler thought, we're getting our tips from a stalker. But considering where they were, maybe this kid really was doing his girlfriend a favour by spying on her.

"Okay," Chris said. He pulled a paper out of his pocket and wrote down his cell number. "Call me when you know they're going to be here again. Are their meetings long?"

"An hour or two."

"Okay. I should be able to get here. Just call. You mind if I get your name and number?"

"Yes," the kid said. "I'll call you. You don't call me."

The limit made sense, and Chris didn't push it. He handed his number over, moved aside, and said, "Thanks for your help."

"Yeah, whatever," the kid said. With one last nervous glance at Tyler, he jogged off, disappearing around the corner of the fence into the industrial park.

"Well," Chris said. "That was strange."

"Pretty crazy chance he would be here just when we were," Tyler agreed.

"No, I mean the way he reacted to you. What do you think that was all about?"

Tyler shrugged. "Maybe I've got an aura."

Chris frowned. "Not the same kind of aura that Wizard guy should have, if he's really into something demonic."

Tyler shrugged. "Maybe he can't tell the difference."

"Maybe," Chris said thoughtfully. He growled. "I wish he'd given us his number."

"He didn't have any reason to. I just hope he calls."

Chris took another long look at the warehouse. "Suppose there's any good reason to stay here? If something really is still going on—I'm just surprised we didn't see anything inside."

"I'm not," Tyler said. His thoughts were a bit tangled, but he tried to unravel them. "The spirit world is invisible, most

     Rachel Starr Thomson

of the time. Even when the core was here, we didn't see or feel them right away."

"Shouldn't you be able to sense demonic activity?" Chris asked. "You or the Lincoln cell? They thought nothing was going on here anymore."

"We can sense things, sometimes," Tyler said. "But maybe not always. Demons can mask. They were working with David for years and they masked it. Blamed it all on Reese, and the Oneness felt something but didn't know what it was."

Chris looked disgusted. "I can't believe any of you fell for that."

"Hey," Tyler said. "I wasn't Oneness back then." He shook his head. "But I don't know how it all works. I mean, yeah, I'm . . . spiritually sensitive, if you want to put it that way. Way more now than before. But mostly just to the rest of the Oneness. Anyway, who knows how much is really going on here? Maybe it's just a bunch of kids fooling around, and that kid freaked himself out. I mean, they were here in the dark, and it's a big empty warehouse."

"But he was reacting to you," Chris pointed out. "Strongly. And he didn't have any reason to if it was all in his head."

"True," Tyler agreed. "But to answer your question, I don't think we're going to find anything more by going back in there right now. It's still just a big empty warehouse as far as we can see."

"Back to the hunt, then," Chris said. He yanked open his truck door and eased himself in. Tyler followed suit, more ill at ease than he really wanted to admit. It did bother him that he hadn't sensed anything in that warehouse when, apparently, some self-proclaimed occult guru could. And it bothered him that the kid had seen them as alike.

You're bothered by a comparison to someone you've never even met, he reminded himself as Chris fired up the truck. Maybe we've got it all wrong and "the Wizard" is Oneness.

Unlikely. But Tyler was unsettled to find how much the idea had blurred the lines in his own head.

* * * * *

By that evening, Chris was growling in frustration. Searching for demons in the city, it seemed, was harder than finding the proverbial needle in a haystack—though Tyler suspected the problem wasn't that they were rare, but that they were everywhere, so normal they were invisible. Somehow he had expected that he would be able to feel them in the atmosphere. But throughout the day he began to suspect that they were always part of the atmosphere here—that he did not know what the world felt like without them. They were there in fear and discord and depression, and in substance abuse and self-hatred and entropy.

After the warehouse Chris just started looking up children's homes, and the pair started off in search of the one interested in Nick. At first they tried to be discreet, act undercover; eventually they gave that up and just asked. Had any home sent personnel to the fishing village? Did anyone have an interest in a boy who lived there—a boy named Nick, suspected to be living in an abusive home, or at least a dirt-poor one where life smelled like alcohol and neglect? In his one concession to discretion, Chris pretended to have information about the kid to pass on. Just wanting to help. His helpfulness accomplished nothing; not one of the homes admitted to being the one they were looking for, and Tyler couldn't sense demons like he'd expected he would be able to.

It was eight-thirty and the sun was going down; they were starving and Chris was frustrated to the point of angry.

Tyler watched the sun sinking over the asphalt and waited for Chris to join him in the truck outside the bank where they'd finally ended up and decided to hang out, in hopes of . . . Tyler didn't know what. Randomly discovering the hive. He wished they'd gone to Richard's work and pulled him out of his cubicle and made him come. Richard with his fasting and prayer and voice of authority really had all the perception Tyler apparently lacked.

Chris had just gotten in, turned on the engine, and flicked the headlights on when his cell rang. He scrambled for it.

"Yeah?"

He started nodding and casting Tyler significant looks, saying "Yeah" and "Okay, right" and "We're coming down." Then he hung up.

"They're back at the warehouse," he said. "You ready to go in?"

Tyler wasn't.

He wasn't at all.

But he wasn't going to admit that.

"Let's do it," he said.

Richard's uneasiness began before he even left work that evening.

Tyler was on his mind. Tyler and April and Reese. All three tied up together like a badly knotted pile of string. A small-town lawyer who primarily handled estates, Richard sat in his office and stared at paperwork he couldn't comprehend for the last hour.

At seven-thirty the notary who shared the office left, and Richard clocked himself out and got on his knees and prayed. He wasn't alone. When Richard prayed he knew the heavens and the ages prayed along with him.

Prayer, as he had once explained to Tyler, was participation in something—it was joining in a continuous song, a continuous work that was humming through the universe all the time.

By eight-thirty he realized what time it was and headed home, so distracted he was sure it wasn't safe for him to be behind the wheel. But he drove on. He wanted to be with Mary. Enlist her help in whatever he was sensing.

He came through the front door still in a state of distraction. The house was quiet. Lamps lit it warmly, casting shadows and creating hollows in the common room. In the kitchen, Mary and April were sitting at the table with Nick. They each had a mug of hot cocoa in front of them, and they were engrossed in a game of Chinese checkers.

Richard allowed himself a faint smile at the sight, but something was wrong. The sense was only getting stronger now that he was with other Oneness. He considered sending Nick to bed on the spot. Then decided against it.

"Quiet night?" he asked, opening a cupboard. Mary turned and smiled. "Yes," she said. But her smile vanished at the look on his face.

It wasn't a quiet night. It wasn't at all. He was sure of it.

April hadn't looked up, and she missed the interaction. "Nick's winning," she announced.

"Good," Richard responded. His eyes were roving the room, seemingly of their own accord. Searching for something. Or someone?

Reese walked in, and for an instant the relief almost choked him. Good. Good, good that she was here.

She asked him a question. He didn't hear it. The Spirit was overriding the flesh. There was still something—

"Tyler," he said.

They turned and looked at him.

"Where's Tyler?"

"He . . . doesn't live here," Reese said slowly. "He's up at the cottage with Chris."

Richard shook his head. "He's not there. I don't think he's in the village at all."

He dropped his earlier hesitation and fixed a gentle but firm gaze on Nick. "Time to get ready for bed," he said.

Nick drew himself up to protest. Richard didn't give him time.

"Upstairs," he said. "Get your teeth brushed and your pajamas on. You can finish your game in the morning."

The boy's mouth snapped shut, and he moved.

That voice of authority again.

As soon as he was gone, Richard looked at each of his worried companions in turn.

"We need to pray," he said. "Something's wrong."

* * * * *

The exterior of the warehouse was as cold and lonely and dark as Tyler had expected it to be. Not a sign of life.

But from the inside, a faint light was shining under the door. And they could hear a low, dissonant sound. Chanting? Music? He wasn't sure.

This time, he could feel demons.

The kid wasn't there. Maybe he had spooked and run off after calling. Certainly the sense of something in the air was strong enough to scare. It wasn't quite like when the core had been here. But in one sense, to Tyler it felt worse. Someone—several someones—were in that warehouse, and they were seeking out the demons and wanting them.

Chris led the way, creeping along the edge of the warehouse wall. He paused near the loading dock door, with the light shining through, and shook his head and kept moving. There was another way in around the back; it was the entrance he'd used when they came to rescue Reese.

Then, they had all been together: Tyler, Chris, Mary, Richard, the twins, and Reese. Reese and the twins were a formidable fighting force; Richard and Mary were another kind of deeper power. They had been hopelessly, hopelessly outnumbered by the core, but somehow they'd come through. Now it was just Tyler, totally inexperienced, and Chris, who wasn't Oneness, invading . . . something.

At least, to Tyler's grim satisfaction, he could feel a sword hilt beginning to form in his hand.

The dark got deeper around the back of the warehouse. The lights of the industrial park didn't reach back here, and they walked in shadow. Chris, ever the natural athlete, moved like a powerful cat. Tyler concentrated on following in his friend's footsteps and trying not to knock anything over in the dark. Chris moved quickly and soundlessly. They found a fire escape and started up it. It led to a catwalk inside the warehouse. Tyler remembered that. He winced with every too-loud step and hoped that whatever the noise inside was, it was loud enough in the ears of the cultists to drown out the sound of discovery.

The door at the top of the fire escape was open, and Chris pushed through with as little noise as possible and held it open for Tyler, pushing it back with his big arm while he faced into the dark. Tyler stumbled through, and Chris flashed him a glance that meant, "Quiet."

Below, the warehouse floor was open to their eyes. As they'd seen earlier in the day, it was largely empty. A few pallets with stacked boxes sat in a cluster near the loading dock door, and another row lined the far wall. The smell of dust and old cardboard were heavy in the air. That, and the faint singe of something that might have been sulphur.

Or that might just be my imagination, Tyler thought.

In the centre of the floor a meeting had convened. They were all teenagers. Tyler thought he counted seven girls and three boys. Plus one—somebody older, taller, with broader shoulders, who was commanding the attention of everyone else even though they were all seated in a circle. Even from up here, his presence was arresting.

Much like Richard's, Tyler thought. And the very idea made him shake inside. He shoved it away.

The Oneness was not like these people.

Chris crouched down on the catwalk, lessening his shadow and the chance that anyone would see him. Tyler bent down beside him. The flickering lights that lit the warehouse came from a circle of candles on the floor. The teens sat in an outer ring around it. They had ceased droning and were listening intently as "the Wizard" spoke. Tyler strained to hear him, but his hushed words were lost in the expanse of space between them.

He ceased speaking, and silence fell.

They started to hum.

Voices that were not theirs joined in. Not teenage. Not human.

Tyler's skin crawled, and without even the usual warning a sword was resting in his hand; he lurched back out of his crouch into a more steady position on his heels, ready for an attack. He felt something like spider legs crawling over his back and neck and he bit back a yell of surprise and fear.

He didn't think he had made much noise, even in rocking back on his heels, but when he turned his eyes back to the floor, the Wizard had turned and was staring back at him.

His eyes were not human.

Something was happening on the floor. A candle flame flared up, and the others snuffed out; a girl screamed, and her scream was picked up and echoed by the other girls, and then they were on their feet and stomping on the ground and jumping like they were trying to crush spiders or avoid mice. The screaming turned to hysteria. Tyler heard a clank of metal and turned his head. Chris was gone.

His knuckles were white on his sword hilt, but he couldn't see where the enemy was or how to fight. The lone candle still burning wasn't enough to light up more than a fairly small circle on the floor, and although shadows jostled around it, it illuminated no one directly. Tyler had seen demons before—he would never, ever forget encountering the core here—but he could see none now.

So what use was this stupid sword?

And where was Chris?

 Rachel Starr Thomson

Frantic, he jumped to his feet and looked both ways. Shadows, just shadows. He ran to the end of the catwalk, reached metal stairs, and started down, bounding as fast as he could without falling headlong in the dark.

When his feet hit concrete, he closed his already white-knuckled hand even more tightly around his sword and charged straight toward the screams and chaos near the candle, pumping both arms and not caring if he ran straight into someone. The sound of something—somethings—scuttling and skittering around the floor met his ears, and something else slithered over his foot. Faint light was coming in from the outside; the front door was open. Shadows were dashing out—teenagers who'd had enough and were running in fear.

Something pushed into his shoulder with a hard, violent shove, and Tyler swung around blindly, throwing a punch that didn't make contact with anything. But the move had him facing the candle again, and now the Wizard was in the light, and so was Chris.

They were facing each other. Chris had his fists up. Both glared.

In the light, and so much closer up, Tyler could see the Wizard's features. He was a good-looking college-aged young man, square jawed and sandy blond. The cloak, black and long and like something from the movies, should have looked stupid but didn't. Tyler couldn't tell what colour his eyes were.

There were shadows, and besides, they still weren't human.

The Wizard said—something—quietly, but with a taunt in tone that even Tyler could hear, and Chris reacted instantly by throwing a punch straight at his face. The young man, easily as tall and probably as strong as Chris, moved impossibly fast and caught the punch. He held Chris's hand in the air for a moment and then started to twist. Chris howled, and his knees buckled. He threw back his head and roared in pain. Tyler grabbed his sword hilt with both hands and hurled himself at the Wizard. Something caught him and held him in place. Frozen. Stuck.

There was a horrific snap, and Chris let out a sound like a wounded lion and clutched his arm to his chest.

The Wizard looked at Tyler, and his unnatural eyes sparkled. When he spoke, his voice had the faint trace of an accent—European, but Tyler couldn't place it exactly.

"Can't fight what you can't see," he said, and laughed.

The last candle snuffed out.

Tyler fell forward and landed on his hands and knees beside Chris. He had dropped his sword—fat lot of good it had done him anyway. He reached out for Chris's shoulder, but his friend lurched away and ground out through clenched teeth, "Don't let him get away."

Like there was anything they could to stop it.

Like they'd had the upper hand for a single minute in this whole night.

The warehouse had gone silent and still. Tyler felt his way across the concrete floor to the wall, using slight light from the open door to guide him in the right direction, and finally flipped on a light switch.

They were alone.

* * * * *

 Rachel Starr Thomson

Chris's arm was broken. Somewhere near the elbow, he thought. He cradled it in the backseat of the truck while Tyler drove for the hospital. They spent only an hour in the Lincoln ER before Chris got taken back for X-rays and then the break was set and given a cast.

Tyler called the village cell house from Chris's phone and told a strangely subdued Mary that there had been an accident, but they were okay and were on their way home.

Before she got off, Mary said, "You know you can't hide, Tyler."

"Whatever," was all he said, and he hung up. He paced in the waiting room while Chris got bandaged up. Finally got a prescription for pain meds filled. Around midnight they were back in the truck and heading home.

"The kid was there," Chris said through gritted teeth.

"What?"

"The kid. The one who told us about the meeting. I saw him before they all ran."

"What do you think that means?"

"It means he lied. All that song and dance about his girlfriend and how he isn't into that stuff himself."

For some reason, Tyler found this hard to process. "Why would he lie?"

Chris sighed heavily. "To get us to crash that meeting."

"Why?" Broken record. But the miles were passing under the truck tires and occasional highway lights, and Tyler didn't find he could think clearly enough to ask anything more intelligent.

Besides, he was unhappy about Mary's parting words. They'd meant he wasn't supposed to keep secrets. He wasn't supposed to hide what he had been doing all day. But these were Chris's secrets, not his. He was Oneness; he loved being Oneness. But Chris wasn't. And he was Chris's friend.

In the back, Chris shifted positions and roared again.

"Pain meds not helping?" Tyler asked once he calmed his heartbeat from the unexpected yell.

"They're working," Chris said, barely unclenching his jaw.

"What did he say to you? Before you tried to hit him?" Tyler asked.

Chris didn't answer. Then he said, "Nothing."

Fine. So they would all have secrets.

"How did he . . ."

"Wasn't human," Chris said. "You see his eyes?"

"Yeah."

"That was a demon."

"Yeah."

They were silent. The city was far behind now; the highway had gone dark. The painted lines of the road lit up as the headlights hit them and disappeared in a high-speed, monotonous flow.

Chris was not Oneness. He and Tyler did not have the spirit connection he shared with the cell and even with the Oneness in Lincoln. But they had been friends for years. Chris had taken Tyler in after his parents died and brothered him through the

    Rachel Starr Thomson

hardest time of his life. And the connection forged in those years was real, and perhaps just as supernatural as anything Tyler was experiencing now.

So they knew much of what the other was thinking as they drove through the dark toward home.

They had both seen demons for the first time when Reese came to them. Two had attacked them. Later they had encountered the core. Demons had run them down on the road and attacked them in their house. They had seen them inhabiting the bodies of animals—birds and bats. They had even seen them in human beings—the thugs who accompanied David had been possessed. But there had been something different about that. Those men had seemed dumb, deaf, absent, and easy enough to deliver from the powers controlling them.

They had not seen a human so perfectly in concert with the demon that possessed him before.

They were equally shaken at having done so now.

A pair of headlights appeared around a bend in the road. A truck, Tyler thought, barrelling down the opposite side of the highway at a speed that was too fast but typical for a night out here. It was a ways off, and Tyler made a note to himself that he was glad it was on the other side of a concrete divider.

Then he realized it wasn't.

It was nearly on him. He swerved.

Then braked.

Blinding headlights.

That was the last thing he remembered.

*　*　*　*　*

The common room in the cell house was still as death.

Reese, Mary, April, and Richard looked at each other with bloodshot, weary eyes, silent in their seats across from one another.

They were uncertain what had happened. But certain that something had.

The Oneness were servants. Fundamentally. And part of their service was war. They warred in more than one way. Sometimes with swords and strategy and skill. Reese had fought that way all her life, alongside the twins and Patrick and others from the Lincoln cell. But sometimes they warred with fasting and with prayer. The latter was not at all what most people imagined it to be. In its most intense and raw it was not much like war at all. It was like being pulled into a current and tumbled through the white waters of a river flowing through jagged mountains and down cataracts, sometimes simply submerged and other times coming up for air and views unlike anything seen from land. This was the warfare in which Richard excelled.

Prayer was surprising, sometimes. They had all seen Chris. And they had all felt Tyler—felt his fear and inexperience and done what they could to make up for it. But they did not know how successful they had been.

In the middle of the meeting, Reese had tried to raise Chris on his cell phone. No answer—not a huge surprise, or necessarily a bad sign, since the phone had bad services and half the time a

　　　Rachel Starr Thomson

dead battery anyway. But it did nothing to comfort them that they couldn't reach the boys.

A knock at the door raised their heads, but slowly, without surprise. It wasn't always easy to come back to the physically oriented world.

Mary stood, but the door opened before she could reach it. Diane came in and hung up her coat on a rack by the door.

"I couldn't sleep," she said. "Apparently neither could any of you."

"We've been in prayer," Richard said.

Diane nodded and pursed her lips. "My boy's in trouble, isn't he?"

"We think so," Mary answered. "He and Tyler."

"What are we going to do about it?"

"We?" The word slipped out of April's mouth before she could stop it.

"Yes, we," Diane said, with a look that tried to be a glare but couldn't manage it.

They were not quite used to having the prodigal back, but it felt good.

"So what are we going to do?" Diane asked again.

Richard cleared his throat. "We're going to try to find the hive."

Diane almost laughed. "Haven't they been looking for it in Lincoln for months already?"

"Yes."

"Then why do we think we can do this when they couldn't?"

Reese answered. "Because Tyler is with the hive. We think. So we have an in. The Lincoln cell never had that . . . and our vision was darkened. Because of David. We didn't know the source of the confusion, but we felt it."

"And when we find it? We aren't the Lincoln cell. Reese is the only real warrior among you. No offence."

"None taken," Richard said. "We aren't going to fight the hive that way. We can't . . . don't forget, the hive is not just demons. It's people. We don't fight people."

"Great," Diane said, making her weary way to the couch and sitting down next to April. "So what do we do with them?"

"We help them," April said.

Diane shook her head. "Why doesn't this feel like a plan of action to me?"

"I'll go back to Nick's mother tomorrow and find out if she knows anything at all about the man who came to her house . . . his name, how to find him. We think he's our first link."

"So we track him down and then . . ."

"And then we see where he leads us, and what they need to become free," Mary said.

Diane raised an eyebrow. "Didn't you come here to get away from this kind of thing?"

"I never tried to run," Mary said. "We had a quiet season. That's all."

Reese smiled sadly. "I feel like I should say I'm sorry."

     Rachel Starr Thomson

"You've had quite enough of that," Mary said, wrapping her arms around the younger girl. "No more. Now, sleep. Everyone. Tomorrow is going to be a sea change for us all. Best we're prepared."

* * * * *

Tyler awoke to the sun in his eyes. This surprised him, and for a moment he wondered why. Then he flashed back, for an instant, to eyes full of headlights, and he realized he was surprised to be alive.

He tried to lift his head and couldn't. It was too heavy. Hands? Arms? All heavy as weights.

He was lying on his back in a bed, but it wasn't a hospital—he was fairly sure of that. No smell of antiseptic, no machines beeping or humming. The light filling the room was all natural; there were no fluorescent bulbs overhead.

The ceiling was stucco, and he could see all four corners from his position on his back. This was a house. He was in a small bedroom.

With concentrated effort he managed to turn his head. Definitely a bedroom. The walls were wallpapered with a blue and white pattern, somewhat Dutch and very busy. Old-fashioned. A bedside table sat next to the bed with a book—a paperback novel that looked like it was supposed to be uplifting and inspirational—and a lamp, which was not on. A glass of water sat untouched beneath the lamp shade as well.

He was horribly thirsty, but he couldn't lift his hand to

reach for the glass. He heard a garbled sound and thought it was himself, calling for assistance.

He didn't really expect anyone to answer, but his door opened, and a blonde head poked in. It was tousled, female, and young—maybe fourteen. Not at all what he expected.

He wasn't sure what he did expect.

Seeing him awake and looking longingly at the glass, she pushed the door all the way open and padded across the floor. Carpeted, he guessed from the total lack of sound.

"Do you want a drink?" she asked softly. It was an entirely feminine voice—sweet and quiet.

He managed a slight nod. Enough to communicate yes. She raised the glass to his lips and gave him enough to quench his raging thirst for the moment. She watched him intently as he drank, her bright blue eyes peering into his face.

With no warning at all, he violently missed his mother.

Rosanna MacKenzie had always wanted another child. In her earnest, never presumptuous way, she had sometimes expressed that she wanted a girl. Perhaps that was why the gut-wrench now—because this young girl on the cusp of becoming a young woman looked like she could be Tyler's sister. But the dream never came true. His parents tried for another child for ten years, and then, in a car accident, they died.

Car accident. Tyler's insides twisted completely around, the paralysis lifted, and he rolled onto his side and dry heaved, gasping, feeling all the physical effects of terror he had not been conscious to feel last night.

The girl ran from the room.

 Rachel Starr Thomson

When the fit passed, he cried.

He missed her. He missed them. So badly. And it had been so long—so many years, and hardly any years at all. Thirteen. Was that possible? Had he lived more than a decade alone?

Chris had been there, his stalwart protector, his best friend. They lived with Diane until they turned eighteen, and then they bought the cottage together and fished as though they didn't know that the world expected more from young men than a life on the water, paying as few bills as possible and never really planning ahead. Theirs was a camaraderie few ever knew; a deep understanding and love they would die for. And yet, all the time, Tyler was alone. Alone in a grief no one else could share.

Until the Oneness.

Until connection, unity, love that was not a feeling but a force, and that force held the world together.

That force had begun to heal things in Tyler that he had spent thirteen years trying to sedate.

But now it was all broken open, all raw, all dry heaving in a room he didn't know in a place that was as strange to him as the moon. The accident had broken it all up and ploughed his soul and cast up stones.

When the sobs he could not control subsided, he realized that Chris might be dead.

This time he did not cry. His resolve hardened and his fists clenched, and he tried to sit and call for someone.

His voice would hardly carry.

But someone came.

The door cracked and the girl came back in, leading a tall, bearded man by the hand. His cheeks were almost pink behind a thick black beard, and his dark eyes were a strange mix of stern and sparkling.

"Lie still," he said. His voice was not loud, but it boomed.

Tyler ignored the instruction and continued to struggle to sit. "My friend . . ."

"Is fine," the tall man told him. "He's resting. Better than you are, I might add." He raised an eyebrow, and Tyler relaxed against the cushions.

"What happened?" Tyler mumbled.

"You narrowly avoided a head-on collision. You missed the truck but not the median. As far as we can tell, your friend was thrown out of the car, and you barely avoided being crushed. We pulled you out. We happened along after the accident. I would guess you weren't out there more than an hour."

"Who are you?" Tyler asked.

"My name is Jacob," the man answered. He lifted the hand that was still being held by the girl. "This is Miranda. The women of our community took care of you most of the night. They're keeping most of us out, but you'll likely have more visitors if you want them. If you don't, just ask them to leave. They'll go. I'd advise you to eat or drink whatever you're given and cooperate with the ladies. They know what they're doing."

Tyler almost asked the question: "Are you Oneness?" But the words wouldn't quite escape. It seemed he shouldn't have to ask that. That if they were Oneness, he would simply know.

And yet, there was something familiar about them.

     Rachel Starr Thomson

And the Oneness didn't always recognize each other immediately—at least he didn't think they did. Diane had managed to live without anyone but Mary knowing for years. Sometimes connection was heightened; sometimes it wasn't. And none of them had been able to recognize the truth about Reese or about David.

Still, the question didn't come out.

"We'll leave you now," Jacob said. "If you need anything, call. Someone will be near the door to hear you. Sleep would be a good idea."

"I'd like to see Chris," Tyler ventured. Weariness, emotional now as much as physical, was pressing him down on the bed. But he wasn't sure he wanted to be alone with his thoughts and memories and aches.

"He's asleep," Jacob said with that curious mixture of sternness and charm in his tone. "As you really should be."

"I'll try," Tyler conceded.

"We can bring you something to help you," Jacob offered. "A tonic of some kind?"

"No, thank you," Tyler said.

"You are already on pain medication. If your limbs feel heavy, that's the reason."

Good to know. The almost-paralysis had been unnerving.

Jacob and Miranda left. In spite of himself—and perhaps because the meds were doing more than just making it hard to move—Tyler slept.

Hive

April winced as she walked up Nick's street to the sound of a couple screaming at each other in a driveway. The woman was drowning the man out, ironically threatening to call the police on the one who sounded like he was just trying to defend himself.

April momentarily considered getting involved, but instead she kept walking, eyes turned away from the couple, letting them work it out. Only their words, their spirits, were violent.

In her joy at getting Nick away from the turmoil in his own home, she hadn't thought about the turmoil in the rest of the neighbourhood. But she was glad, now, that he wasn't here listening to the stream of profanity flowing from the woman's mouth, and soaking up the general sense of hopelessness, anger, and chaos that characterized this place. For the most part the fishing village was quiet and peaceful; people weren't wealthy, but neither were they poor, and most inhabitants had chosen to live here, chosen the lifestyle and the view against the cliffs.

This block, and another one street over, constituted the only really rough section of town.

Shelley was sitting on the cracked concrete of her front step. She was despondent and almost certainly drunk. When she saw April, she frowned as though trying to remember who she was and then said, "Did you bring my kid back?"

"No," April said quietly, sitting down on the step next to Shelley like she belonged there. "He's really happy at the house. You should let him stay a while."

"He's a good kid," Shelley said.

"Yeah, he is."

"He deserves a good mother."

April almost said, "He's got one," but she stopped. She wanted the words to be true. Shelley tugged at her heart almost as much as Nick did. But she wasn't really sure she could tell her, even for the sake of compassion and in hope, that she was a good mother.

Shelley let out a long groan and leaned her head back against the doorpost, and they sat like that for a minute, looking down the street toward the bay and letting the humid breeze cool their faces. The smell of salt hung heavy in the air, weighing down April's lungs even as it made her feel more alive. Overhead, the blue sky was flawless. The sun shone down on cracked curbs and no sidewalks, grass growing too high in yards and dented metal garbage cans that had been left out after the last pickup day. Like most environments, the street reflected visibly the invisible things of the hearts that lived on it, and engrained them more deeply. It fell apart because these people had so little pride, so little care, so little dignity. But how could they, when they lived here? Catch-22.

   Rachel Starr Thomson

"So what do you want, anyway?" Shelley asked abruptly.

April hugged her knees to her chest. "Well, I was wondering about that man. The one who wanted to take Nick away."

Shelley eyed her suspiciously. "You change your mind? Going to send Nick there after all?"

"No, no. I wouldn't do that. I want Nick living with me." April hesitated. "I just wondered if you knew anything about him. Did he tell you his name?"

"Yeah," Shelley said. "Some kinda doctor or something."

"A child psychologist, you told me," April reminded her. "Did he say where he was from?"

"Lincoln," Shelley answered. Bingo.

"And his name?"

Shelley grimaced. "Dr . . . something."

"Do you remember his first name?" April prodded, hoping for anything to go on.

"Started with a V. Sounded Italian or something." Shelley laughed. "Vino."

"Maybe Vincent?" April guessed.

To her surprise, Shelley looked surprised and nodded. "Yeah, yeah, I think so. Dr. Vincent . . . something not Italian. Smith."

Great, April thought. Probably a pseudonym.

"Did he say where he was from? The name of the children's home, I mean?"

"Can't recall," Shelley said. "It was long."

"I see."

April tried to stem her rising frustration. Maybe Smith wasn't a pseudonym. Maybe they could track him down using that name. Her eyes roved over the driveway, recalling the car sitting there, wishing desperately she had the kind of perfect recall that could pull up a make and model and license plate. All she knew was it had seemed like it came from a bygone era. Oh—another flash of inspiration struck.

"What about the kids?" she asked. "He had two kids and a woman in the car with him. He say who they were?"

"No," Shelley told her. "He just left them sitting out there. I offered to let them come in and have a drink or something."

April frowned. It was a whole lot less than she had hoped for. At the least she'd been optimistic that Shelley would turn out to be a talkative drunk and would let loose some clue, but the opposite seemed to be true.

"Well, thanks," she said finally. "I should probably go."

"Wait," Shelley said. Without a word of explanation she got up—steadying herself on the doorpost—and disappeared inside. April stood and waited uncomfortably, shifting her feet. The couple down the street had quieted for a few minutes, but their volume was rising again. At least it still didn't sound like anyone was actually being physically threatened.

Shelley reappeared in the doorway with a small bundle wrapped in a plastic bag. "It's Nick's favourite shirt," she said. "It was in the laundry when you came."

With unexpected tears in her eyes, April accepted the bag, said good-bye, and started home.

          Rachel Starr Thomson

Once she got off the street, the fight grew too quiet to hear. It was replaced by the occasional car passing, the sound of TVs inside open screen doors, the call of gulls overhead, the distant lapping of the bay. A quiet weekday in the village. Children were laughing somewhere. But April found the sounds dissonant. Because on Nick's street a woman was still screaming at her man, and Shelley was still drunk and still too lost to be a mother.

April's feet dragged the last few blocks to the cell house, and not only because she was tired.

"Vincent Smith," she announced when she entered the kitchen. Reese looked up from a pot of something on the stove.

"Dr. Vincent Smith. Sound like a real name to you?"

"Could be," Reese said. "At least his first name isn't John."

"I'm not sure it's Vincent either," April said, sitting down with a wince. She tossed the bundle of Nick's shirt on the table.

"You all right?"

April leaned her head in her hands. It ached. "Yeah."

"You are still supposed to be taking it easy," Reese said. "Building up your strength. Not walking all over town."

"Thanks," April said, "but I'm okay. Really. I just want to do something."

Reese sat down across from her. Strain showed in every line of the young woman's face. "I know. Me too."

April reached out and touched Reese's hand. "You care a lot about those boys, don't you?"

"They rescued me," Reese said. "Both of them. And they weren't even Oneness."

Chris still isn't, April was going to point out, but thankfully she caught herself and said nothing.

April and Reese had not talked much since they both came back to the cell house and began living together. Both had been through hell because of David. Both had exposed him. Both had nearly died doing it. But the experiences were too personal for words, and they stayed silent and simply felt the commonality between them.

The commonality, and the gap.

Reinstated in the Oneness, Reese was. But somehow, since her exile she had not come fully back to trust. And April's near-starvation and isolation had done something to her as well. She had wounds that needed healing. Maybe she was afraid that getting too close to Reese's still-raw hurts would only reopen her own.

"So," Reese said. "Dr. Vincent Smith. I'll call around and see if I can find him."

"Shelley said he came from Lincoln."

"I assumed that."

"You think this is all connected to the hive?"

Reese didn't answer or nod, but she leaned back in her chair and squinted her eyes like she was putting memories together. "We never did find the hive itself. We found its core—the place where demons were gathering, empowered by David."

She stopped.

April bowed her head. David's betrayal of the Oneness, peaking in his exile of Reese when he thought she was too close to discovering him, was the evil the demons had thrived on. The

     Rachel Starr Thomson

evil powering everything they faced now. She thought again of the couple screaming at each other in Nick's old neighbourhood. There was no such thing as a small betrayal of love.

It was, in fact, the sin that threatened to destroy the universe. The primary evil that the Oneness existed to combat.

Reese went on. "It created a demonic core in an unused warehouse in Lincoln, and from there they went out and possessed—building the hive. We knew it was happening, sometimes encountered some of the victims, but we never really cracked the hive itself or found a way to locate all its members. I thought that attacking the core would undo it. It might have worked. But the exile happened."

She paused again. "And then you happened. Your kidnapping. And you got this village involved."

"Actually," April said, "I think you did that. If Tyler and Chris hadn't found you, and cared so much about what happened to you, the connections might not have been made in time."

Reese shook her head with an opaque smile. "It's a good thing I don't have to understand how the plans work."

"Do you think they're real things? Plans? Or is that just what we call life after it happens and seems like an unchangeable, a given?"

Reese squinted again, taking time to process that. "I think they're real things. How else could you have painted prophecy all over that cave wall?"

April shrugged. Her memories of her time in the cave were odd. Not at all dim—she remembered every waking hour with a vivid clarity most of her memories could not claim. Yet they seemed unreal for all that. Like an especially vivid dream, or something that had happened outside of this world completely.

"Do you think plans ever fail?" April asked.

Reese looked at her curiously. "Are you always so frivolous?"

"I almost starved to death," April said. "It affects your thinking."

Reese smiled. "It helps if you were a thinker to begin with."

"You didn't know me before."

"I can guess at you before."

April laughed. "Probably accurately."

"I don't know," Reese said plainly. "For a while there I knew I was caught in a plan—David's. The hive's. I don't know if the enemy can override the Spirit and trump God. I just don't know."

"I think," April said, frowning, "they can't. But I wish I knew."

"Sometimes you can't know. Or we can't, anyway. Our perspective is too limited. So we can only trust. Or so I tell myself."

"You still struggle with it, don't you? The exile. It still hurts."

"It remade me," Reese said simply. "Not in ways I like. I hope I can heal more than I have."

She shook her head as though to dislodge that thread of conversation. "I'll start calling around to see if I can find this children's home of yours. Do we have anything besides the name—Smith—to go on?"

"No," April said, blowing out a breath of frustration. "Nick's mother was drunk, and I'm not sure she really learned anything about the home even when she was sober. He just walked in and played off her guilt and intimidated her into almost giving up her son."

April looked off into the distance out the kitchen window and shuddered.

Whatever Reese had on the stove started to rattle, so she got up and clicked off the gas element. "Egg?" she asked.

"Sure."

Nick appeared in the kitchen entrance, solemn and silent. April wondered if he'd been standing in the common room, listening. She regretted having mentioned that Shelley was drunk.

"You hungry?" Reese asked from the stove.

"Yeah." He crossed the floor and sat down at the table like he knew he belonged there. April smiled. "What have you been doing today?"

"Went fishing off the pier with Richard," Nick said. "Caught nothing."

Reese, listening as she sawed off a couple slices of bread and dropped them in the toaster, said, "You should go out on Tyler's boat sometime. The fishing's better out on the water. They would teach you."

Bless your optimism, April thought. Reese knew as well as she did how very much the enemy played for keeps. Who knew if Tyler and Chris were ever coming back?

The thought made her wince, and she realized that if she were Reese, she would refuse to consider it.

"There isn't much to do around here," Nick announced.

"I'm sorry you don't approve," April said.

"Oh, I like it," Nick answered. "But you need more things to do."

"Do you have something in mind?"

"Yes," Nick said, and he drilled April with his intense blue eyes. "You can teach me to draw."

April drew back, startled. How did he know she could draw? She hadn't shown him.

A slight shadow of guilt passed over his face, but he didn't seem to think it worth hanging onto. "I found your sketchbook," he said. "You're very good."

Recovering her composure, April said, "Do you like to draw?"

"Yes," Nick said, leaning forward, "only I've never really done it—but yes, I know I do. I just need to learn."

Old soul, April thought. And kindred spirit.

"I can teach you," she told him. "There's an art store by the water . . ."

"I know," he interjected.

". . . we'll go buy you some paper and pencils. Now, if you want."

"After lunch," Reese cut in, setting down a plate in front of each of them. Toast and eggs.

 Rachel Starr Thomson

"This is breakfast food," Nick pointed out.

Reese stuck out her tongue. "It's the only thing I know how to cook."

But Nick's comment hadn't been criticism, more just an observation—as was clear from the energy with which he tucked in. April watched him eat, amused even as her heart ached at the memory of his mother, and the thought of how often he'd probably gone hungry, and at her own memories, of lack and alcohol and parents she wasn't sure had ever loved each other. The little boy across the table had a right to be old for his age. Just as they were kindred spirits for several reasons.

Her memories still hurt, and in many ways they still made her who she was. But for April, everything had changed when she became One. Her childhood had become, not a cancer determined to destroy her over the course of her life, but a ploughed field receptive to new seeds, new life. The Oneness had gathered her into its pulsing heart, its arms that were the universe and the Spirit at the centre of the universe.

Through her, those arms were reaching for this child. And something in his spirit, she knew, was answering.

Deep calling to deep. The beckoning, and the rising up to follow.

Nick finished his scrambled eggs, and April stood. "Come on," she said. "Let's go."

Reese gave her a look as they went, a silent promise to make those calls right away and know something, anything there was to be known, by the time April got back.

"Why did you go see my mom?" Nick asked as they walked

side by side down the quiet street toward the village. The air had grown full-out muggy and hot, and gulls overhead sounded irritated and crass in their calls. No breeze carried coolness off the water toward them.

"I thought she could help me with something," April said.

"No, she couldn't," Nick said flatly. "She can't help anybody with anything. Not me, not my dad, not you."

April felt the accusation like a slap in the face. She'd known Nick harboured bitterness. But she hadn't known specifically toward whom or what. That it was his mother felt worse, somehow, than if he had just been angry toward his circumstances or even toward his father, who April knew he barely ever saw.

"She can't even help herself," Nick went on. "She's worthless."

April stopped dead in her tracks and stopped Nick with a hand on his shoulder. He pulled away but didn't keep walking, glaring up at her defiantly. Guiltily.

"That's not true," April said. "No one is worthless, Nick."

"Then why doesn't she do anything?" he burst out. "She needs so much, and I need so much, and she doesn't do anything about it. Nothing."

"She isn't worthless," April said again. "She's hopeless—without hope. That's a different thing."

Nick turned away and stared down the road at the bay. She could see emotions boiling up in him, threatening to overflow in a burst of energy like she'd seen so many times from him: running through the streets or along the docks, riding his bike

     Rachel Starr Thomson

straight down the steeply sloping road like he would fly off the end and pedal madly through the sky itself, swimming until he exhausted himself. This, too, she understood. She had taken up running as a young teen to avoid the edge of all she felt. To channel it into speed and pain and muscle. But she needed him to not run right now.

"Nick, when people can't see hope, it's like not having light," she said. "They feel stuck in the dark and they can't see any way out. Your mom is like that. But she loves you."

"She can't take care of me," Nick said, and April knew exactly how much that blunt confession meant in his world.

"It's true," April said. "But she sent you to live with us, and not with that man from the city. He probably put some real pressure on her, you understand that? She did something brave by sending you to us."

Nick started walking, straight down the hill toward the art store near the harbour. April sighed and followed after him. Together they descended to the flatter ground at the base of the cliffs, a forest of masts and sails, with the blue of the bay stretching out beyond it dotted with white sails and the occasional white caps of boat wakes. A row of slightly upscale shops lined the richer side of the docks, with a pub punctuating one end and a coffee shop the other. Next to the coffee shop the art store sat, its doors wide open, smelling to the discerning nose like possibilities.

Nick hesitated before he went in. He looked back apologetically. April smiled and nodded, wordlessly forgiving him for his anger and giving him permission to go in. She had often seen him hanging around the shops by the water, but not going in.

She doubted most of the shop owners would mind him hanging around, but he had limited himself.

He hung back slightly until she reached him, and they both went in past a street display of journals and sketchbooks into the store itself. The walls were painted in swirls of pink and green, and bright display shelves lined them. More art materials and how-to books were placed on wagons acting as tables in the centre of the floor. It wasn't a large space, but the owner had managed to make it feel breezy and open and inviting.

Nick was casting nervous glances at the proprietor behind the counter, despite her welcoming smile, so April stepped in, trying to hide how tired she felt. "We're looking to get a budding artist supplied," April said.

"Pencils or paints or both?" the proprietor asked. "Or some other medium?"

"Pencils," April answered, "and a good sketchbook. And anything else you recommend."

She checked Nick to make sure his expression was approving of the order, and to her relief it was. She would be happy to teach him to paint, but maybe not quite yet.

The proprietor, a young-looking middle-aged woman in tie-dye, came around the counter and directed Nick to the sketchbooks, showing him several and talking his ear off all the while. April smiled and stepped back, letting her mind drift to Reese and her search for the elusive children's home. She offered up a prayer that the search would be successful.

Armed half an hour later with four sketchbooks in various sizes, two so big that Nick had to hug them to his side with his arm, and pencils, pastels, and charcoal, they stepped back out onto the boardwalk along the dock. The scents of coffee and fried pub food mingled with salt and seaweed. It was cooler down here by the water than up the hill, and April soaked up the warmth and the beauty of the day. Nick's step was noticeably lighter, but neither spoke as they wandered through the marina, in no hurry to go back home.

On the other side of the marina's main offices and a restaurant, a pier stretched out into the water. Nick pointed. "That's where me and Richard fished."

"But you didn't catch anything, huh?"

Nick wrinkled his nose. "Naw. We'll try again. Maybe tomorrow. I don't think Richard knows much about fishing."

April laughed. That was probably true. Richard was a lawyer by day and a man of prayer by night, born in some city far away and only come to this village because the Spirit's mysterious ways had directed him here. For that matter, none of their cell really belonged in a place like this. They weren't like the Sawyers, tied to the water and the land by nature and long acquaintance.

"When do you think Chris and Tyler are comin' back so they can take me fishin' for real?" Nick asked.

Was he reading her thoughts? "Soon, I hope," she answered.

"Something bad is happening, ain't it?" Nick asked.

She regarded the small boy sadly. "A lot of bad things go on in the world," she said. "We just try our best to make what we can right."

"Yeah, well . . ." he looked down at the pencils in his hands and the sketchbooks wedged under his arm. "You do a pretty good job."

* * * * *

From the light outside the window, Tyler guessed it was late afternoon when he awoke again. He wanted to get out of bed. His limbs still felt heavy, but not quite like before. He examined himself, more alert this time, and found scratches and bruises but nothing that looked severe enough, in his opinion, to justify keeping him here. And he still hadn't seen Chris.

Feeling for some reason like a rebel, he struggled to sit up and then get his legs over the side of the bed. To his consternation he discovered he was wearing a long white nightgown. True, considering the collision his clothes were probably in rough shape. But these people could have had the decency to put him in shorts.

Walking was harder than he thought. He'd made it halfway across the room in the direction of the door and was leaning with one hand on the wall, panting, when the door opened and a woman came in, disapproval written all over her homely, middle-aged face.

"Now," she said. "Jacob told you to stay in bed."

What, were you eavesdropping? Tyler thought, but he didn't ask. Neither did he budge from his position on the wall. Truthfully, being on his feet was harder than he'd expected, and he was not sure he could stagger back to the bed, much less out the door.

The woman didn't seem to care. She marched over, took Tyler's arm, and half-prodded, half-steered him back into bed. "Now then," she said, "Jacob told me to find out if you're hungry. Are you?"

"Umm," Tyler said. "No."

Her frown was enough to prompt a retraction. "I could eat something," he said. "But not much."

"That's better," she said. "I'll bring you supper."

"How is my friend?" Tyler rushed out before she could disappear.

She stared at him as though he were out of line. "The big guy," he continued. "The one I came here with."

"He's fine," she said abruptly. "He's getting lots of sleep and eating, like you should."

Aware that he wasn't going to get anything else out of her, Tyler settled back into the bed and resigned himself. At least if he ate, he would be one meal closer to getting strong enough to get out of here completely.

A breeze stirred the curtains, and he wondered when the windows had been opened and what he would see outside if he could get over there. All that was visible from the bed was blue sky. He thought he heard chickens clucking and maybe the far-off sound of some kind of farm equipment. He couldn't hear or smell water, which made him unhappy. Tyler had always lived on the bay. Being inland made his feet itch.

He strained his ears for sound outside his room but could hear nothing, confirming his suspicion that he was in some far-off upstairs corner of a house. And he found himself wondering again if these people could possibly be Oneness. On the surface they looked like it. Jacob had mentioned "the women," so it wasn't just a family house. And Jacob himself had had an aura—a powerfully attractive sort of charisma that in a way reminded

Tyler of Richard. The sort of aura that spiritual power gave off.

Thinking of Richard made Tyler realize that he hadn't been able to communicate with anyone in the village, and if they had figured out that he and Chris hadn't come home last night—or whenever exactly the accident had happened—they would be worried. He made a note to ask for a phone when the woman came back with his supper.

He had a definite impression that she thought of him as a pesky little boy, so he might as well pester some more.

His mind went back to the original question. Were these people Oneness? No, he decided. If they were, he should be able to sense connection with them, to know them, and he didn't. And yet . . . he doubted himself. He was still new at this, and he was drugged up and probably injured. And there was something about these people. If it wasn't Oneness, what was it?

His desire to talk to Chris galloped back up again, and he blew out a breath of frustration at his failed attempt to reach the door. Whatever they were giving him for pain, he wished they would stop it. At the moment he would prefer a little pain to being unable to stand without a wall to lean on.

The woman came back, pushing the door open with her hip while balancing a tray of food on the other. Apparently they weren't going to overstuff him—the tray contained a steaming clear broth and a small plate of crackers. Tyler was pleased to find he was hungrier than that, and simultaneously annoyed that they were babying him. He tried to muster enough consternation to protest, but all that came out of his mouth was, "So, um, I'm Tyler."

The woman glared at him. He wondered if she knew how

to smile. "Lorrie," she said shortly. Then she drew herself up a little and continued, "Jacob is my husband."

What was he supposed to say to that? Congratulations? "So is this your home?" he asked. "I mean, do you own this place . . . this . . . farm . . ."

Apparently the drugs were affecting his ability to speak intelligently too.

"No," she said. "The community owns it."

"The community?" Tyler asked.

"Five families," she said. "We live here together and keep ourselves separate from the world. Farm the land, raise our own food."

Apparently that question had pulled out the plug.

She nodded toward the window as though Tyler could see anything through it other than clouds. "We farm about twenty acres. Expecting a good crop this year. Everybody works hard to provide for everyone else. That's how it should be."

It suddenly occurred to Tyler that these people were doing him a service, even if they were only feeding him broth. He felt ashamed of his impatient attitude. "Thank you," he said, and meant it, "for helping me and Chris. I don't know where we'd be without you."

She looked at him like he was an idiot, but he thought he detected a slight softening around her eyes. "You'd be in a hospital, most like."

"So why aren't I? I mean, why didn't you just call an ambulance?"

"It's not our way." She thought better of the abrupt answer and went on. "We don't involve the world unless we have to. This time we didn't have to. Neither of you are hurt that bad. Eat your supper, you'll be out of here soon."

Unlikely, Tyler thought, as long as you keep feeding me various forms of water. But he didn't say that out loud. Obediently he picked up the spoon and maneuvered soup clumsily into his mouth, pleased to find that the broth was deceptively flavourful and made him feel stronger and more clear-headed after only a few bites.

Lorrie left. He still wanted to see Chris.

Closing his eyes, Tyler tried to reach out for the Oneness. To feel the connection with the great community that stretched across the earth and in some way held everything together, like a web of threads creating a tapestry. He felt . . . he wasn't sure what he felt. No clear connection with any other soul; no contact, so to speak. But he felt a conviction, a settledness in the pit of his stomach, that said he was not alone and that he was centred in something far greater than himself and that something was love and strength.

It was more than enough.

He found that he was tired by the time he finished his soup and ate a couple of crackers, and he fell asleep.

When he awoke, a committee had seated itself in his room.

At least, that's what he thought at first. Their serious expressions, folded hands, and air of discussion gave that distinct impression. They reminded him of town council meetings in the village, which he had occasionally attended with Chris when something was going on pertaining to fishing regulations.

        Rachel Starr Thomson

With a slight jolt, however, he realized they weren't exactly human.

There were six of them, and he couldn't tell what they were sitting on. There were no chairs, but they were definitely sitting. They were all a little too big—too tall and too broad—to be human, and with two of them, he couldn't quite make out whether they were male or female. The rest looked male. He thought.

The real clincher was that he could see through them.

They were talking. The biggest of the group said, "The Oneness has often expressed itself in communities like this."

"Then what makes this one different?" This was a smaller one, younger maybe. "Why is one community a ground for evil, and another is a place of health and growth?"

"The difference is Spirit. A community based in the Spirit is free at the core. And others are bound. Love makes free; fear binds. What comes of a community like this depends on what's at the centre, but that is not always obvious from the outside."

"It's obvious to me," another commented.

The big one looked witheringly at him. "Because you can see things they can't. That is not their fault. They are as God made them to be."

"And that is why," one said in a tone of awe, "they can love."

Tyler was not sure whether the beings just vanished or whether he woke up from a dream, but either way the room was quiet, just a breeze stirring the curtains, and there was no one there.

What in the world?

Maybe it was the drugs, he told himself.

Or maybe not.

He wished Richard was here so he could ask whether trans-lucent, now-you-see-them-now-you-don't committees were a normal part of life as Oneness. Richard would know the answer to a question like that, and if they were a normal part of life, he would be able to explain why and what it meant when they showed up.

But Richard was not here, and he had forgotten to ask about a telephone.

Determined anew not to keep going alone, Tyler forced his legs out of bed and staggered across the room. This time no one interrupted his sojourn. He cracked the door open and peered into a hallway. Empty. He wasn't sure how he was going to find Chris or a phone—either one would do at the moment—so he just kept staggering on, out into the hallway, one foot after another, with his eyes and ears open. He felt like a guilty child up for a drink after he'd been put in bed and expected a stern parent to interrupt him at any moment. But no one did. Apparently he'd escaped while everyone was busy.

The hallway was typical for a country house built toward the earlier end of the century; narrow, with several rooms open-ing off of it on either side. He listened carefully outside of each door for some sign of Chris's presence. Said sign nearly hit him in the nose: one of the bedroom doors opened into the hall at the same moment Tyler was leaning toward it for a listen. He jumped back, uncomfortably tipsy on his feet, just in time to avoid being smacked by it. And Chris staggered out.

     Rachel Starr Thomson

Chris looked considerably worse than Tyler did, or at least worse than Tyler thought he did. His arm was still in a cast, but the cast looked dirty and beat-up, and "beat-up" was the best description of how the rest of Chris looked too. He was banged up and scratched and bruised, and even less steady on his feet than Tyler was.

None of which stopped him from grabbing Tyler in a huge, wordless bear hug. They leaned on each other for a moment and then both staggered backwards and let the walls hold them up.

"Good to see you too," Tyler said. "You look rough."

"You're not exactly pretty yourself. Where the heck are we?"

"On a farm. Somewhere."

"We should be in a freakin' hospital."

Chris was angry. Tyler frowned. He'd been irritated at their rescuers, but he'd mostly chalked that down to the combination of drugs, trauma, and inconvenience, not to any actual bad calls on their part.

"They're not taking bad care of us," Tyler said. "They don't like hospitals."

"They Oneness?" Chris shot back. "That why you're taking their side?"

Tyler pulled back. "Hey, come on. Nobody's an enemy here."

As an afterthought, he added, "I don't think they're Oneness. They could be. Maybe."

"Shouldn't you know that?"

Tyler shook his shaggy head. "I'm new, all right? I don't really know what I'm doing."

Chris groaned and leaned even more of his body weight against the wall. "My everything is killing me. I want to get out of here and go home."

"I thought you wanted to go to a hospital."

Chris's eyes glimmered. "Because they're understaffed. They would send us home."

"So the problem with these people is, they're taking too good care of us."

Humour finally sparked in Chris's expression. "Something like that, yeah."

He looked Tyler over with new interest. "You hurt?"

"Achy," Tyler said. "Bruised pretty good. But nothing serious. I don't think. They've got me on some pain killer and it's messing with my head."

"You seem pretty normal to me. You've always been a dope."

Tyler managed a punch. "Takes one to know one."

Chris looked around. Both ends of the hallway ended in a blind corner. Presumably at least one had stairs around it. "Come on," he said, hauling himself off the wall with another groan. "I want to find a phone."

On the march down to the end of the hall, Tyler wondered what had happened to Chris's cell phone. Most likely crushed or lost in the wreck, he thought.

Oh, the truck. He hadn't even thought about the loss of the truck. That was going to be a pain to recover. He hoped Chris

     Rachel Starr Thomson

had good insurance.

Tyler had never really been the one to deal with that kind of detail.

The hallway was wallpapered with a striped, pale pink and blue pattern, and Tyler trailed his fingers along the stripes as they walked. The corner was sharp and the stairs down narrow, and the wallpaper gave way to something hideous and flowered that didn't match the stuff upstairs at all. He wondered how many years this house had stood and how many clashing tastes had wallpapered parts of it.

The stairs ended in a square room on the ground level with one small, high window. The room was lined with shelves full of empty canning jars. Its door stood just slightly ajar. Chris pushed through without hesitation, and they stood in another smallish room, this one furnished as a sitting room. Windows looked out on a pleasant green day, but the aspect was overshadowed by the roof of a porch. Tyler felt cramped and wondered if the house ever really opened up. The cottage he shared with Chris was tiny, but it always seemed a part of the cliffs and the sea and the sky. The village cell house had been purposely bought and then redesigned for space: the large common room was meant to bring a community together, even though the village cell was so small. They had always planned for more than they had. And in prayer, Tyler thought, maybe they met with more than were visible.

He wondered if the common room ever played host to committees.

That room was empty as well, but by now they could hear voices in another room, and a door swinging and banging against its frame. Chris led the charge. In the dank atmosphere of the house, Tyler thought unexpectedly of being boys together, chasing monsters through the cliffs. Chris had always been the one to lead.

But Tyler doubted they would find any more monsters here than they had ever actually found in their boyhood.

Another door led them into the kitchen and a flood of light. The room was far more open than anywhere they had been in the house; Tyler suspected it had been an add-on. An open kitchen with three industrial-size fridges and lots of counter space, including a central island, opened onto a dining room that was just as large. A big oak table looked like it could comfortably seat twenty people, and a few smaller tables off to one side seemed designed for younger, smaller people. Tyler briefly checked for wallpaper, just out of curiosity. Both kitchen and dining room sported a bright yellow chicken print, but the feel was much more modern than anything upstairs.

Ten women were up to their elbows in suds, bread dough, or huge bowls of mixed ingredients. They had been talking; they stopped when the boys entered the room and exchanged glances. Their expressions confused Tyler: unease, disapproval. One glared at him, and he recognized Lorrie.

"We wondered if we could use the phone," Chris said.

"We're up," Tyler added, kicking himself inwardly. Well, that won the award for completely unnecessary statement of the day.

"We're glad to see you're feeling better," one of the women said. She spoke softly, almost hesitantly, but Tyler thought she meant it. She was younger than Lorrie, maybe thirty or a little

     Rachel Starr Thomson

older. He thought she looked a lot like Miranda, the girl who had visited him with a glass of water when he first woke up. All the women wore long skirts and aprons, and they wore their hair long and tied back. They looked like something from Little House on the Prairie.

Lorrie was much more down to business. "You can't use the phone," she announced. "We don't have one."

Chris blanched. "You don't have any?"

"We came here to get away from the world," Lorrie answered. "Telephones are just a way to bring the world in."

"What do you do in an emergency?" Chris pressed. "What if you have to call 911?"

"We don't have to do that," Lorrie answered. Tyler thought the younger woman was about to say something, but she evidently thought better of it.

"Seems stupid to count on that," Chris said. "Nobody counts on accidents."

Tyler looked askance at his friend. Apparently being in a wreck had made Chris even more bearish than was usual lately.

Or maybe he just really wanted to see Reese.

"If we had an emergency, we would deal with it," Lorrie said, her voice frosting over even more. "We do take care of our own as well as strangers, Mr. . . ."

"Sawyer," Chris said, his answer to the pointed inquiry a clear capitulation. "Listen, I'm sorry if I was being rude. We just need a way to reach family and let them know we're all right."

Lorrie was still looking at Chris like he was something

distasteful dragged in from the outside—from the world, Tyler thought—but she answered, "I'll talk to Jacob and see what we can do. Now, we had best get back to our cooking." She shot the other women a look that said they'd all dallied long enough. "And you young men had best go back to bed. You don't seem to believe it, but your bodies took quite a beating in that accident."

Tyler realized like a lightning strike that he hadn't even thought to ask. "What happened to the truck driver?"

"Oh," Lorrie said, "He's here too."

*　*　*　*　*

Not half an hour later—the younger woman from the kitchen insisted on feeding Chris and Tyler more soup before they actually obeyed Lorrie's injunction to get back upstairs— both boys were sitting in the bedroom where the driver was asleep, clearly medicated and just as clearly in far worse shape than either of them. He was not old. Tyler guessed late thirties, maybe early forties. His face was a square-jawed, flat-browed rectangle, with several days' worth of dark growth on his cheeks.

He moaned and shifted under his sheets, and Tyler and Chris exchanged a worried glance.

It appeared the driver had received a great deal more care than either of the boys. One leg was in traction. It was carefully splinted and bandaged, even expertly so, but likely needed a cast. The man's head was also swathed in bandages, and it looked like part of his head had been shaved to treat a cut along the back and side of it. The room smelled of antiseptic and something else Tyler couldn't place—something herbal, he suspected. The scent was sweet and almost cloying.

"They should take him to a hospital," Chris said, his voice strained. He was holding some emotion in check. Probably anger.

Or possibly fear.

"Or call the police," he continued. "What kind of people spirit all the victims out of a car wreck and don't tell anyone?"

"How do you know they haven't?"

"Because if the police knew about this, they'd have been here. To write up an accident report if nothing else. And he would be in a hospital where he belongs."

"I don't know," Tyler said. "I think these people are doing their best."

Chris raised an eyebrow, but this time he didn't explode. "It's good to give people the benefit of the doubt. But you're giving them too much benefit."

"How do you know? It seems like they know what they're doing."

"I just don't like how isolated they are," Chris admitted. "It doesn't feel right. Or . . . safe."

"Safe? What danger do you think is here?"

Tyler asked the question in earnest. As much as he wanted to defend this community, Chris wasn't the only one who sensed some danger lurking here. But he couldn't name it.

"Like this," Chris said, encompassing the room and the unconscious driver with a gesture. "Who knows how badly hurt this man really is? I believe they're trying to take care of him, but what can they do without X-rays, or scans, or whatever? He could be dying. They wouldn't know."

Tyler pensively watched the sleeper. He didn't look like he was dying. Just uncomfortable. Then again, his sleep might be a coma. And his face was ashen.

"It's not safe for them either," Chris went on. "All those women down there. If something was to happen to this guy, like he died because he didn't get the right medical care, all those women would be implicated in the death."

"Your problem, Mr. Sawyer," said a third, unexpected voice, booming into the room and and making both boys jump, "is that you seriously underestimate our medical knowledge and ability to give care. And, I might add, you judge our policies without really knowing what they are."

They turned. Jacob stood in the doorway, looking on both of them with an expression that was not exactly a frown—more like the smug sternness of a schoolteacher who had caught the biggest troublemakers in the class red-handed.

He strolled into the room, hands in his pockets. He wore hardy work pants and a striped, button-up shirt that was sweat and dirt stained. Cleary he'd just come in from the fields. "The women told me you had some questions," he explained. "First off, several in our community are trained medical people. One MD and two RNs, in fact. They are capable of telling broken bones and signs of serious internal injury—and of discerning between a coma and sleep. He is sleeping, and he will wake up. We're helping the sleep with a little something, because rest will heal him. We have, in fact, filed a police report. And if the situation warranted—which it does not—we would move him to a hospital. We are not careless."

Chris's mouth gaped as he looked for an answer, but he didn't find one fast enough. Jacob's next words startled his thinking off track anyway.

"After dinner, which I suggest you join us for since you're so clearly on your feet, you can use the phone to call whoever you like. I'll have the ladies bring you up some decent clothing."

"I thought you didn't have a phone," Tyler blurted.

"Not one for general use, but we keep an emergency line. My wife was overzealous in denying you access to it. I've talked to her about that."

He turned to go. "When your visit with our driver here is over, consider yourselves invited downstairs. Clothes will be waiting for you in your rooms. The family is coming in for dinner, and it's a good opportunity to see our community as it actually is—not as you conjecture it to be, hmm?"

Tyler and Chris exchanged a wordless glance when Jacob had stepped back out of the room. They were almost afraid to talk. Apparently the walls around here had ears.

Although the walls had also, Tyler conceded, had some comforting things to say.

He wasn't sure why he didn't feel comforted.

Chris whistled. "I guess I got told."

Tyler grinned, but it was halfhearted. "I guess you did."

"Too bad our friend here wasn't awake to hear it. He'd be glad to know he's getting such good care."

"I believe him, though, about all their training and stuff. They seem to know what they're doing. And somewhere they've gotten a lot of meds," Tyler said. Still not sure why he wanted to defend these folks.

"Yeah, well, I guess. Except I think he's lying about the police report part."

Chris stood. "Not that I blame him. If was in his position, I'd lie too. About that."

* * * * *

Dinner was charming, homely, odd, and disconcerting—all at once.

When the boys made it back downstairs—stopping for a rest after they got dressed, as they were still weaker and more tired than either of them wanted to admit—most of the community was already indoors. The whole ground floor smelled like soup. Chicken and vegetable, with garlic and parsley. Fresh bread added to the delectable smell. Tyler found himself wishing for more solid food—he couldn't get excited about soup after all that broth he'd been sipping—but suspected his stomach might not handle it well anyway. Children were everywhere, but well-behaved for the most part. A pair of boys were wrestling on a throw rug between the tables, but one of the adults quickly put a stop to it. There were more than half a dozen adults, most of them younger than Jacob and his wife. All were dressed alike: long skirts and aprons for the women, work pants and button-up shirts on the men. Beards were in strong supply. Lorrie had said there were five families, and that seemed about right, with lots of children between them.

          Rachel Starr Thomson

They were, in a way Tyler had not encountered before, beautiful. In their set-apartness was a sweetness and wholesome innocence that made him want to argue against Chris's impressions even more, to insist these people should just be protected and honoured.

When the meal was called to order—literally, by Jacob, who sat at the head of the main oak table—everyone scurried to his or her spot and stood at attention. Jacob led in a formal prayer, and everyone sat down at once. Tyler wondered if he might miss part of the choreography if he didn't pay attention. And then he almost did—he reached for a bun from a bread basket in the middle of the table and drew his hand back just in time to avoid being the only person making any sort of move toward the food. All eyes were on Jacob instead.

"Nathan," he said, fixing his piercing eyes on a young man about twenty-five who might have been his son, "tell us about your day."

In measured sentences, Nathan did. He talked about work in the field and recounted something innocent and amusing that had happened with a ground squirrel. Everyone laughed, especially the women, whose eyes twinkled and shone.

Next Jacob called on another young man, and then on Miranda, and then on the woman they had met in the kitchen, the one who might be Miranda's mother. Her name was Julie.

Each of them gave a similar story: work, something amusing, and then sometimes, tacked on the end, a lesson they had learned. The stories showed the sweetness in these people that Tyler liked. But there was a weird formulaic quality to them that set him on edge.

Equally strange, to him, was that no one cut in or interrupted or grabbed the ball of conversation and carried it in any new direction. They spoke only when called upon by Jacob.

Fair enough, Tyler thought; if everyone in here talked at once, it would be chaotic.

But alive, in a way that this wasn't.

He silently rebuked himself for judging and tuned back in.

"Tyler," Jacob said, making him jump, "tell us about your day."

Tyler's face grew hot. He had not expected to be called upon and was not sure what he would say.

And he knew he was expected to follow formula, and he didn't want to.

"It was fine," he said. "I'm getting stronger. Thank you all for your care."

And that was all. He couldn't tell if he had offended. But really, how could he have followed the formula even if he'd wanted to? He hadn't worked, he had no funny stories about animals or small children, and the only moral he'd learned was to ask Jacob for permission to do things, not Lorrie.

Jacob stood, stretched out his hands, and gave a formal blessing upon the food and upon all those who sat at the table. When he sat back down, dinner commenced. So did general conversation, though it was quiet and surprisingly subdued, especially that coming from the children's tables. Two mothers were serving, so they hovered over those tables and probably had a lot to do with how hushed the kids stayed.

For some reason Tyler thought of Nick throwing himself off

     Rachel Starr Thomson

the dock. And then of himself, as a child, wrestling through all the enormities of death and trying to live again. He wondered if these children ever had to wrestle with anything, and if they did, how they found room to do it.

Dinner was good—enormously satisfying, in fact. Tyler suspected his meds were wearing off. He was beginning to be in more pain, and it made sitting uncomfortable, but his appetite was coming back. Not a bad trade-off, he decided. If his pain got too bad he'd take a Tylenol. At least that would allow him to walk in a straight line.

When the hardworking community had finished dinner, the young men eating three bowls of soup in the time it took the women to eat one and some bread, Jacob cleared his throat.

Everything fell to an immediate hush.

"We are privileged to have guests with us," he said, "hearing and seeing our way of life. I think they're still a little resistant to our ways, but let's all pray they come around." Humour twinkled in his eyes like that was supposed to be funny, but Tyler's face heated up again. Jacob resumed his speech without waiting for any response from either of the guests. "When we came out here ten years ago to escape the world and serve God and one another in simplicity, we faced a great deal of opposition from people who insist on following their own selfish, worldly ways. Persecution is not always easy, but it makes us stronger. Even amongst us, sometimes, there can be pressure to return to more culturally acceptable ways of doing things." His expression burned, and Tyler suspected he was speaking to one or two in particular. Thankfully he didn't call them out by name. "It's up to all of us to rebuke those who err and remain faithful to our calling. The world is always at the gate, trying to lure us back in. But I hope we all remember how tawdry and wicked the world's ways truly are."

Tyler found himself with the urge to raise his hand and ask exactly what "ways" Jacob was referring to, but he didn't. Something about the whole speech was making him uneasy. From the way Chris was fidgeting, he didn't like it either. Maybe it was the implicit way the two of them were being identified as "of the world" and therefore dangerous.

You don't actually know us at all, Tyler protested silently, aware that several eyes were on him. I wouldn't call the Oneness worldly. Or culturally acceptable. And Chris—well, Chris was just Chris. Beating a path all his own like he always had done.

But the next thing Jacob said startled Tyler so much he nearly fell off his chair.

"It's important for us always to remember who we are," he charged his little community. "We are walking the true paths of God, in unity and simplicity. We are Oneness."

Tyler's protests drowned in a swamp of sudden confusion. He had known there was something different—spiritual—about these people from the start. They lived together like a cell and clearly took care of each other. They weren't like the world.

They said they were Oneness.

Were they?

He was still trying to figure that question out when he and Chris went to the phone, in a small shack on a corner of the property, and tried to call home. The phone rang and rang, and Chris tried calling twice, until giving up after thirty minutes and storming inside.

* * * * *

Richard stood alone at the end of the pier, watching the sun set over the bay. Light touched water in a royal display of brilliant purple and orange. But at the moment, what his eyes saw mattered less than what he felt, what his spirit heard when he listened closely.

In the Oneness, every individual had a gift all his own. Many assumed Richard's was prayer. He spent hours in it; he drew strength from it; he gained insight through it. But they were wrong. Prayer was not a special gift for specific individuals. It was an open door to all, an invitation into the deeper things of reality. It was like an ever-flowing stream, thought and sight and strength of the Spirit itself, and anyone could plunge into the depths. If they would.

But few did.

Young in his life as Oneness, Richard had determined to go in prayer as far as he could. He had been twenty-one, sober and serious but far too given (in his own opinion) to flings of fancy and wild self-indulgence. So he reacted as extremely as he could think to react: he denied himself food for forty days and forty nights and went out into a wilderness to pray. For that long month and ten days in June and July he camped in a tent in the mountains and learned how to listen, how to be carried away. It wasn't like that at first. For more than twenty days he did not listen but talked, at first in his mind and then out loud when the silence drove him crazy. Realizing he had not come out here to listen to himself, he stopped talking for another three days and desperately tried to negate himself, to shut off his mind altogether so he could tap into the vast Unconscious. Boredom had been an issue even while he was still talking; now it threatened to derail the whole enterprise, and anyway, he couldn't do it. The words and images that are a human mind do not turn off.

Then finally he realized they were not meant to, and that to pray was to converse; back and forth, talk and listen, give and take. He found new awareness of a stream that had been flowing around the whole time and took the first few truly exhilarating steps into discovering what it meant to be carried by that stream.

When he got home, back to the mid-size city cell where he'd been born into the Oneness, many treated him like a hero and a mystic, and it was silly. He still didn't really know what he was doing. He hadn't learned anything of substance; he had just begun to learn how to learn. That realization kept him humble, and still kept him humble, even though now, twenty-five years later, he had actually learned a few things and was more comfortable in the strange rush that was prayer than anyone he knew.

The orange on the water deepened, burnt and glowing, and the sun began to sink beyond the horizon.

Richard could feel the participation of others who were Oneness in the stillness, like vibrations along a vast symphony of strings. Some only skimming the surface. Some diving deeper than even Richard knew how to go. Prayer was a song, a continuously rising composition that had played for thousands of years, in heaven and on earth, and would play still when everyone he knew had passed into the cloud and taken up a new part in the music.

To stand on the edge of the water and feel the subtle strains was to delve into a peace that transcended events and circumstances.

Prayer did not always give actual answers.

But almost always, it gave peace.

Richard breathed deeply of the salt air and focused his heart on Tyler and Chris, on Reese and April, on Nick, and on the mystery of the battle they were fighting. Who and what and where and why—everything one should know before going into a fight—were blanks, or guesses. What exactly David had created and how it was affecting their lives now, he could not say.

But he prayed. The music groaned in his soul.

He lifted the groan into words, heavy, simple. Asking for help. It was not a flowery prayer. Those who truly prayed rarely did so verbosely.

A throat cleared behind him—some way back, but he heard it. He turned and smiled.

"Hello, Mary."

She approached, glad for his permission. "I didn't mean to interrupt."

"Then I will consider this a joining, not an interruption."

"Fair enough." She sat down on one of the concrete posts of the pier, looking out over the water and the sinking sun. The air was still warm, still enveloping.

"Have you learned anything from the Spirit?" she asked.

"Only the usual."

She smiled. "All shall be well."

"Yes."

The smile faltered, and she sighed. "Little help at the moment, though."

"I think it's a great help," Richard said. Not combatively, just telling the truth. "If I didn't think that things were going to turn out right, I'd go hide under a rock, not fight this fight."

"Reese called every children's home in Lincoln today, but she couldn't find a Vince Smith."

"Not that surprising."

"No, but disappointing anyway. It would feel good to have something to go on."

"Do you feel like the boys are in danger?" Richard asked.

"I don't know. Do you?"

"Not . . . exactly. Something isn't right. But the urgency of the other night has lifted. Chris has been chewing nails to get after the hive. I suspect they went hunting."

"A little strange that they haven't contacted us."

"They've been independent for years. Maybe it's not that strange."

"Tyler isn't independent. Not anymore."

"And Chris doesn't like it. Tyler may just be keeping the peace."

"I wish he would join," Mary said quietly. "I worry about him. He's joined this battle and he isn't armed for it. They could take him down so easily."

"But they haven't. Maybe he's not so easy to take down as you think." Richard's eyes twinkled. "Maybe the sides aren't quite that black and white."

"They could be a big puddle of grey for all I care. All I know is that if they encounter the demonic, Tyler is green and Chris can't fight."

"But then again, Chris is better in a fistfight any day. And at least some of what they may encounter should be vulnerable to fists. Don't borrow trouble, Mary."

The sun disappeared, but its last rays still lit the sky and the water. Richard held out an arm. "May I escort you home?"

When they turned together, they could see the lights of their home high up the hill. So obvious, so clear. And yet the village had never really seen them, or known them for what they were: guardians, peacemakers, servants of God.

Lights flickered high overhead, and Richard saw them and smiled.

Most people would have said they were stars coming out, or passing airplanes.

He knew them to be angels.

And the watchword of the Oneness came to mind:

Never alone.

*　*　*　*　*

When Richard and Mary walked in the front door, half an hour after leaving the bay and meandering up the road in the twilight, Reese greeted them with the words, "I found him."

"Who?" Mary asked, caught off guard.

"Dr. Vincent Smith. Who is either using his real name or consistently giving out the same fake."

"I thought you'd already called around?" Mary asked.

"I did," Reese answered, handing them both a cup of tea. She'd had a pot ready, clearly intending to ambush them before they could just go to bed. "In Lincoln. But it occurred to me to call some of the outlying communities too. He's from Brass, an oily little town fifteen miles north of the city. The Lincoln cell used to do double-time keeping watch out there, but it's been quiet lately."

"So what have you learned?" Richard asked, accepting his cup of tea and moving into the common room. He and Mary arrayed themselves on the big leather couch; Reese positioned herself across from them. The rest of the house was quiet.

"Well, he does run a children's home," Reese said. "Just a small one—ten kids. And he and his wife have two of their own, which the woman I talked to thought was a selling point. Seems the home was an outgrowth of fostering."

"Nothing scary so far," Richard said.

"Not on the surface, no," Reese admitted. "The woman gushed about his credentials and his wonderful way with the kids."

"That doesn't sound much like what April encountered."

"Yes," Reese said, her eyes glimmering, "but you know

appearances." She leaned back and sipped her tea. "I thought I would pay them a visit tomorrow. Better not to take April, since she's already encountered him—and the demons he's carrying. If nothing else, I should be able to get a feel for what's happening there."

"What do you suspect you might find?" Richard asked carefully. Mary's eyes were downcast, as though she didn't really want to fully engage in the conversation. Hives were horrible enough. Involving children made it that much worse.

"It could be an expression of the hive," Reese said. She took in Mary's expression and cast her own eyes low, staring into the steaming cup. "I hope not. I hope we just find one man under demonic influence and we can do something to free him or mess up their operation. But it fits the profile. A home, where everyone is contained, under the leadership of a charismatic individual. Kids can be really vulnerable, especially if they come from broken backgrounds."

"You sound like you've had experience with hives," Mary said.

"Not really. We only fought the core. The human side was always just beyond our finding it. But once we realized there was one stemming out from Lincoln, I learned all I could about them."

Her voice quieted. "I've been looking for this thing for three years. Since I was nineteen. It nearly cost me everything. I wouldn't be honest if I didn't tell you I'm scared of what I might find tomorrow."

Mary rested a hand on Reese's knee and said nothing.

Reese let out one more sigh. "And the children . . ."

"You'll do right," Mary said firmly. "You'll know what to do, and you'll do it. You're Oneness, Reese. One of our best."

Reese blinked away tears and squeezed Mary's hand.

Richard stood slowly. "I am going to pray," he announced. "Do you want anyone with you tomorrow?"

"Yes," Reese said firmly. She set her cup down. "That's the other thing I wanted to talk to you about." She squared her shoulders. "I want to take Diane."

Tyler didn't know how long he'd been asleep, or how long the man down the hall had been groaning before the groans awakened him. But he snuck out of his room and down the hall and into the dark bedroom, wary of meeting any of the community. No one seemed to be around. Either they were ignoring the man's wordless sounds, or they had already checked on him, or they didn't care.

He rebuked himself for the last thought. These people might be strange, but from everything he had seen of them, he knew they cared.

This late at night, newly awakened from sleep, Tyler found all his emotions about the community were at the surface, sublimating his conscious thoughts. Jacob and his people attracted him, fascinated him, and repelled him all at once. He felt at once inspired by their example and condemned by it. He didn't know what to do with the mix.

It was too dark to see when he stepped into the room at first, but a moment later a cloud slipped off the moon, and moonlight streamed in through the window. Tyler could make out the shape of the man in the bed and his leg suspended in the air.

Apparently the man saw him too, because he startled so badly Tyler thought the traction apparatus was going to come down.

"Who's there?" he choked out, frantic.

"It's okay, it's just a friend," Tyler said, moving himself into the moonlight. "My name's Tyler. I heard you . . . just wanted to make sure you're all right."

Maybe it was partly due to the shadows, but to Tyler it seemed fear was etched across the man's face. He calmed down slightly as Tyler came closer, but the fear remained, lurking, palpable.

"Where are we?" he asked.

"With a community in the country . . . somewhere." It bothered Tyler a little that he still didn't know the answer to that question exactly.

He wondered what else the man didn't know, so he kept talking to find out.

"You were in an accident. You were driving a truck and you nearly hit us head-on . . . you were in our lane. Do you remember any of that? But we're okay. We avoided you and hit the median, but we're fine. Just a little bruised up."

The man shook his head. "I don't know what happened. I picked up a hitchhiker. We were talking—just small talk. That's the last thing I remember."

"These people—here in this community—found us all

     Rachel Starr Thomson

and took us in. They've been taking care of us. They've got you bandaged up good."

"I seen some of them," the man acknowledged. "I thought I was in a hospital. My head's been so fogged up. Just woke now and . . . why aren't we in a hospital?"

Tyler shrugged. "These folks don't so much like the outside world, and they figure they're good enough at caretaking. Seems like they're right."

He didn't bother mentioning the supposed police report. Chris had thought that was a fabrication, and he was probably right. Oneness cells did not typically like to involve police, he thought, remembering April's disappearance and the fact that Richard and Mary had never called in the authorities.

Of course, an inward voice corrected him, in that case they hadn't called in the police because they figured the event was demonic, and they didn't want to get non-Oneness humans wrapped up in it. The car wreck was not demonic.

Was it?

His interest in the events of that night suddenly rekindled, Tyler asked, "Do you remember anything about that hitch-hiker?"

"Sure," the man said. "He was freaky. Had the craziest eyes I've ever seen. College kid, I think."

Tyler sat up straighter. "Do you remember what he said?"

"Naw," the truck driver answered. "Nothing much. Just the usual chitchat . . . where you from, where you going, that kind of thing. I tell you one thing, we sure as anything weren't driving on the wrong side of the highway. But that's all I remember." He shook his head and stretched his neck in frustration. "It's like I had a seizure or something. Maybe I did."

"Hey, I'm not trying to stress you out," Tyler said. "I can let you go back down to sleep. Just wanted to make sure you're okay. You were groaning."

"I hurt," the man said. "Feel a little better now. Thanks."

Tyler stuck out his hand. "You have a name?"

"Rick Brodie."

"Good to meet you, Rick. Tyler." He'd already given his name once, but this was more formal. He wasn't sure why he didn't give a last name. Oneness generally didn't. He hadn't made a conscious decision to take up that practice, but somehow it just felt right to use his first name only.

"Sorry I woke you," Rick said. "Listen, can you find me some more pain meds or something?"

"I'll try," Tyler told him.

He headed down the dark hallway wondering where on earth he would find anyone to give Rick more medication. This wing of the house didn't seem to be home to anyone other than the guests.

In the dark, he almost bumped into a small, quiet form. She gasped loudly, and his heart raced.

"Hey, Miranda, sorry."

"That's okay," she whispered, breathlessly.

"I was just up checking on Rick—the driver. He wants something for pain. Can you . . ."

"I'll tell Lorrie," she said. For some reason she sounded

 Rachel Starr Thomson

scared. "Has he been awake long?"

"I don't think so, not too long," Tyler answered. "Why . . ."

"I was supposed to be up here listening for any needs," Miranda said, "but I got hungry and . . . don't tell, will you?"

"What, that you were gone for a few minutes?"

"Yes. Just don't tell."

"Okay," Tyler answered, confused. There was a pause during which Miranda might have given him a smile or a look of gratitude—it was too dark to see, but he felt like she was grateful—and then she turned and vanished back down the hall. He felt his way to Chris's room.

"Chris, wake up," he stage-whispered when he got inside.

Chris didn't move.

"Hey, Chris," Tyler said a bit louder, ambling to the side of the bed and poking his friend.

Nothing.

Alarmed, Tyler bent down to make sure Chris was still breathing. He was—regularly, deeply. Since when did Chris sleep so well?

Normally he slept with a proverbial eye open, ready at any moment to stand down the attack of the world.

Bothered but tired and achy, Tyler went back to his own room. He sat in the dark and thought, I should pray.

He didn't really know how.

It would have been nice to have spent more time mentoring with Richard before getting thrown out on his own like this.

Thrown out? his contrary inner voice contested. You walked into this one yourself.

He cleared his throat. What exactly were you supposed to do when you prayed? As a kid he'd always been taught to close his eyes and bow his head. But things were different as Oneness—really, really different. He didn't think most other people had prayer right at all.

He cleared his throat again. He wasn't sure why he was doing that, either. Was he planning to speak out loud?

Prayer is participation, Richard had told him once. You enter into the river as it passes by. The Spirit is always praying. Just jump in.

But I can't hear what you're saying, Tyler protested. I don't even know how to listen.

Being quiet might be a good start, said his inner voice. At least trying to hear something else.

Fair enough. He cleared his throat again—annoying himself—and shifted position on the bed and tried his best to be quiet.

He wasn't sure how long he continued with that before he fell asleep.

*　*　*　*　*

Reese left early in the morning. Richard donated his car for the purpose, opting to walk to work. April and Mary and Richard all got up to see her off. And Nick.

Nick looked particularly concerned as he watched her pack a lunch and pull on a light jacket. He stopped her on the way out the door, lurching forward and grabbing her sleeve.

"Be careful," he told her. Fear was dancing in his eyes.

"No worries," she told him, meeting his gaze as sincerely as she could. "I will."

The drive to Diane's house was short. Reese rapped on the door and tapped her foot nervously in the damp air. Fog on the water obscured the bay, opening to a grey sky far overhead; it looked to be a wet, drizzly day. Not that one could ever really tell in the morning what the rest of the day would look like.

A fine day for demon hunting, she thought. The war always seemed so incongruous on beautiful days.

She lifted her fist a second time and rapped again on the door. She had called Diane last night and asked her to go to Brass. More argued than asked, actually. And she knew the whole time she talked how horribly unfair she was being. Diane would have refused anybody else outright. But it was Reese asking. Diane was worried about Chris, and Chris and Reese clearly cared for each other, and well, how could a mother's heart say no? Reese felt a tiny twinge of conscience for using Chris like that, but it was important to her that Diane learn to be Oneness.

It had, after all, been Diane's face that pulled Reese out of the grief that was swallowing her and turning to anger and vengeance. It had been Diane's face, at the last, that turned the tables and prompted Reese to spare David's life. She still marvelled that they'd won that battle. Hopelessly outnumbered, and with half of them injured, they should have died there. Ultimately she knew it was her forgiveness, her letting David go, that had beaten the demonic core. Fighting demons was not just a matter of swordplay; it was a matter of love, of rightness, of making choices that they would never make—of creating wholeness and building bridges when their whole bent was to corrupt and rot and destroy. Other battles, with equally bad odds, had been fought and won by similar decisions. But it was impossible to manufacture a moment like that. And in the moment, she had not known what was right.

Not until she saw Diane's face.

She knocked again, louder this time. It finally opened. Diane stood there, wearing dress pants and an oversized beige sweater. All ready to go.

"Sorry," she said, but she did not offer an explanation for what had kept her.

She had probably been sitting in the kitchen on the other side of the door, telling herself not to go.

"I packed us a lunch," Reese said, making conversation as they crunched the gravel on the way to Richard's car. It was a nice car, a whole lot more luxurious than driving Chris's truck.

But Reese paused just before she reached for the door handle and wished she was riding in Chris's truck anyway.

On the drive to Lincoln, Reese noticed deep tracks crossing a grassy median like someone had fallen asleep at the wheel and crossed to the wrong side of the highway, and before that, black marks slashing a concrete divider like there had been a collision.

"Nasty accident there," she commented, uneasy at the thought. From the tracks, it couldn't have happened more than a day or two ago. Right about the time the boys went missing.

But Richard didn't think they were in danger. She held on to that. Besides, if Tyler was dead or badly hurt, one of them should feel it.

She hoped.

He hadn't been with them long enough. Had the ties formed deeply enough to really tell them anything?

Shaking her head to dislodge the thoughts, she kept driving.

Diane was a sullen passenger, staring out the window and hardly saying anything. Reese thought about turning on the radio to cover the awkwardness—Richard's car probably had good sound—but didn't. They drove in silence.

In Brass, the house wasn't hard to find.

They stepped out of the car, and Reese felt the familiar stench in the air and the presence of petty forces scrabbling over dominance in a kingdom almost too small to care about. She had described the town as "oily" when she told Mary and Richard about it, but perhaps "burnt" would have been a better word. A plant on the edge of town poured smoke into the air all year-round, smogging up the air. A thriving little drug trade empowered most of the demonic activity in the town. The Lincoln cell had made plenty of raids here, looking for weaknesses, finding people who were ready to be helped out of the nets they'd become entangled in. But it seemed there was always someone to take the place of those who were rescued.

Reese never stopped being amazed that the human race could be so set on destroying itself—and for so little reason.

This was a nicer part of the town than she had been in before, and the house was a decent size—the size of two or three typical houses, actually. The yard was large and showed signs of use: she caught sight of a volleyball net out back and a few toys were strewn across the walk to the front door. She quieted herself for a moment and listened for some sign of something more than human here—for the familiar buzz in the air, the smell, the sense of tension.

They weren't there.

Frowning slightly, she waited for Diane to step up beside her.

"What do you think?" she asked.

"What do I think? I think it's a nice place," Diane said.

"I think so too. Which is . . . strange."

"Come on," Diane said, starting toward the door and stepping over a plastic truck. "Let's get this over with."

Reese found herself following Diane, smiling slightly. Diane might not want to be here, but she WAS here, and ultimately it had been her choice—unfair tactics or no. Even her bad mood was more indicative of a lost fight than of any intention to keep trying to stay separate from the Oneness. That battle was over, and Diane knew it.

She had gone to find April while the others fought their battle in the warehouse. On the wall she had seen April's mural—the story of David and the hive and the betrayal of Reese. Maybe seeing David like that, realizing what a whole-hearted effort to separate oneself from love and community really looked like, had scared Diane into her new openness.

Whatever; Reese was just glad she was here.

They reached the front door and Diane knocked, looking, Reese realized, a lot older and more professional than her

     Rachel Starr Thomson

companion. Diane might have been a social worker calling on business; Reese, in jeans and a sweater, looked more like a recent children's home graduate herself.

The door was opened by a woman whose tentative inquiry as to who they were transformed into a smile as soon as Reese mentioned that she had called the evening before.

"Oh, come in!" she said, swinging the door wide to a prettily decorated foyer, with a mirror, end table, and vase of flowers as its centrepoint.

"I'm Susan Brown," the woman said. Reese stopped herself from commenting. Brown and Smith? These people might all have taken their names from a collection of pseudonyms. Susan was a woman of average height and build, with bobbed brown hair and friendly eyes. The warmth she exuded seemed genuine. She paused and indicated the closet if either Reese or Diane wanted to hang their sweaters up, but when neither did, she led them through the house, chatting brightly. Several teens were seated at the kitchen table, dressed for school and eating breakfast. Susan introduced them, and they said hello more or less dutifully. A boy about nine years old was sitting in the midst of them, holding court and obviously amusing two of them to no end. An even smaller girl, five or six, ran in from the dining room and waved, then dashed back out.

"Those two are Dr. Smith's children," Susan explained. "The Smiths both live here and oversee the work, as well as working individually with the children to help counsel and guide them. I'm the extra house mother—with ten to twelve kids at any given time, an extra mother never hurts!"

She went on, ushering them through the kitchen, dining room, and two family rooms. A wide carpeted staircase led upstairs, and she indicated most bedrooms were up there. Reese and Diane nodded and occasionally said hello to one of the kids. It was becoming fairly evident that Susan thought they were here because they were interested in contributing to the work somehow.

"We are a privately funded organization," she said finally, when she had brought them back around to the kitchen. "We operate mostly on donations, although Dr. Smith does bring in some of our funding through his practice. As you can see, our aim is not just to give the children a home, but to help launch them into a stable and productive future. Now, would either of you like a coffee or tea?"

Reese said yes to coffee, and Diane asked for a tea. Susan turned to open a cupboard, calling over her shoulder, "Children, the bus! Finish up and get going!"

A few stragglers in the nearby living room jumped at her summons, but it seemed most of the kids were already heading out. The overall feel of the house was much like Susan herself: orderly but not at all tyrannical, as warm and genuine as it was structured and organized.

Reese had to admit she was impressed.

She sat down on a tall stool next to the counter and leaned forward, trying to sound nonchalant. "Is Dr. Smith in today?"

"Oh yes," Susan started to say, but her eyes caught sight of someone else over Reese's shoulder. "Excuse me," she said, and then raised her voice. "Alex! You're going to miss the bus again!"

Reese twisted in her seat to see a dark-haired young man, dressed in torn jeans and a black T-shirt, slinking down the stairs. He all but ignored Susan, rolling his eyes slightly and neither

     Rachel Starr Thomson

speeding nor slowing his pace.

"You know better than to go out in those jeans," Susan called. "Dr. Smith's not going to be pleased."

The kid muttered something in response that didn't carry past the stairs; hefting a backpack higher on his shoulder, he jogged the last couple of steps and pushed his way out the front door.

Just before he left, he turned and looked back inside.

His eyes locked with Reese's.

And filled with terror.

A second later he was gone, and Reese was half out of her seat.

Had she imagined that?

Fear . . . why was he afraid of her? He'd never seen her before. Knew nothing about her.

The answer came without further thought. Yes, the fear was real. And no, he had never seen her before.

But the creature inside him had.

And it could see exactly what she was.

Maybe they'd found the hive after all.

Susan was talking. Diane nudged Reese. She snapped her attention back to the women in the kitchen.

"I'm sorry, what were you just saying?"

"Oh," Susan said, looking after the boy with a frown, "I'm sorry about that. Most of our kids here are so good, but Alex . . . well, he's having a hard time. Some really do when they hit their teens. Dr. Smith has been putting a lot of extra effort into trying to help him. Oh, but I was answering your question. Dr. Smith is at his office right now—he always goes in very early—but he'll be here later today if you'd like to come back. He's always happy to meet with potential new supporters and introduce them to more of what he does."

She lowered her voice to an almost conspiratorial level as the coffee machine behind her started to percolate. "If you ask me, all his psychological training doesn't have a lot to do with how effective he is. What he really does for these kids is just father them. He loves them, and they know it. That makes a world of difference for most."

There was sadness in her tone. Diane leaned forward and placed a motherly hand on Susan's, surprising Reese. "You're doing the best you can," she said. "It's not your fault that boy isn't responding like you want him to. Sometimes we just have to figure things out for ourselves."

True, Reese thought. But this was not the conversation she'd imagined them having when she got out of bed this morning. She realized suddenly that she'd half-risen from her seat, wanting to go after the boy. But the sound of air brakes outside told her the bus had come. He would be gone.

"All the children attend the local public schools, high school and elementary, except one who goes to a private school where they're better at dealing with special needs. All three schools are good ones, and we have a good relationship with several of the teachers. They know what we do here and work with us as much as they can. Most of the children are in summer school programs right now, since most need remedial schooling when they come to us."

"Tell me," Reese said, still distracted but trying to focus back in on the conversation, aware that she might miss something that was actually important to putting the pieces together, "if you could sum up the mission of this home in one word, what would it be?"

Susan smiled. "Why don't I let Dr. Smith answer that?" she said. "You may be the first person who's actually asked that question unprompted, but he answers it all the time anyway. And he does a better job than I would at explaining the one word. What do you think? Can you come back this afternoon? Or stay? You'd be welcome to stay."

Reese got the feeling this wasn't a usual invitation. Susan seemed to have warmed to them both; her invitation wasn't polite, it was eager.

"I think we can stay," Diane said. She raised an eyebrow at Reese. "We don't have another appointment until later, do we?"

"No," Reese said. "Sure, we'll stay. Thank you."

She felt vaguely guilty for taking up the woman's time when it was unlikely either she or Diane would end up as financial donors, but Susan seemed so pleased at their acceptance that it wiped away much of the guilt. Her interest in them didn't seem primarily financial anyway.

The house, emptied of children, was quiet, and Reese heard the hum of a garage door opening. "Oh, Valerie! Good!" Susan said. She got busy pulling out an extra mug and pouring more coffee. "Valerie is Dr. Smith's wife and the other counselor here," she said. "She'll just be getting back from taking Sandy to school . . . she's the deaf teen I told you about, the one who goes to a private school."

The inside garage door opened and an attractive, professionally dressed woman stepped in. Blonde, styled hair and a perfectly tailored blue suit made her every inch the professional, but there was nothing superior in her expression as she approached and shook Reese and Diane's hands, greeting them warmly before Susan had even had a chance to introduce them.

"This is Diane and her daughter, Reese," Susan said. "They're interested in our work here, and I just invited them to stay until Vince gets back."

"Sounds great," Valerie answered. "I'm glad you're here. Do you like what you've seen so far?"

"Yes," Reese answered truthfully, not bothering to correct Susan's impression about her relationship with Diane. She did like everything she had seen.

All except the demon in one boy's eyes.

But how to fit that with these people and everything else about this place, she had no idea.

Dr. Smith held the key. He had to. After all, it was he April had seen and faced off at Nick's house—he April had actually rescued the boy from.

Standing here, now, that was incredibly hard to believe.

Valerie stood and chatted for a minute more, exchanging a bit of information about the deaf student with Susan and then remarking again on how glad they were to have Reese and Diane visiting, and then excused herself to spend some time with her daughter before a counseling appointment.

"Dr. Smith and Valerie live upstairs in the left wing," Susan explained. "They have a few rooms converted into a complete apartment so their family has some ability to separate from the rest of the house when they need to. It's good for their kids, I think, especially since they're so much younger than most of the others."

Reese noticed that Susan viewed the home kids as just "others," other kids, other children, not students or subjects or some other category of human that didn't quite equal the status of the Smith kids. April had told her a story or two about being fostered and how, in one home, she had felt like some other species of human than the foster family. The more she saw of this place, the more she liked it.

Dr. Smith, she reminded herself. Dr. Smith will hold the key.

"Well, ladies, please make yourselves comfortable," Susan said. "I need to make a few phone calls from the home office and then I'll be out again. If you need anything, don't hesitate to knock—the office is just down that hall."

Susan vanished, leaving Reese and Diane to their coffees and each other.

"Well," Reese said.

"This is nothing like you expected, is it?" Diane asked.

"That might be an understatement."

"You're sure you don't have the wrong place?"

"How many Dr. Vincent Smiths, specializing in child psychology, can there be near Lincoln? This has to be the right place. I think we'll know more when we meet him."

Diane huffed into her coffee cup but said nothing.

Moments later she emerged and said, "I don't think this

is going to get us closer to Chris. But I think he'd like it here. He's such a protector, and these people seem to really care about these kids."

"I'm sure you're right," Reese answered quietly.

"Be careful with that son of mine," Diane told her. "You know you have his heart."

Reese swallowed hard and nodded.

"But you won't give yours in return, will you? Because he's not Oneness?"

"Diane . . ." Reese struggled for words. "You haven't walked with us, or acknowledged us, for a lot of years. But you know what Oneness is. Surely you do. Surely you understand why I can't just pretend that doesn't mean anything."

She lowered her voice as though someone else was listening, as though anyone else in this house would know or care what they were talking about. "I care about Chris, a lot. He and Tyler saved me. Not just by pulling me out of the bay—they gave me a reason to fight and a reason to believe in love again. I can't overstate how much that means to me."

"And Chris is special," Diane pushed. "There's something between him and you that isn't there between Tyler and you."

"I can't argue with that. But it can only go so far."

Diane looked away.

"Please understand," Reese said. "He already has my heart—in some way. I just don't know what that's supposed to look like. In the real world, here where we all have to live."

"You could push him to convert, or whatever you call it," Diane said. "Like I should have pushed my husband and didn't."

"Would he really have responded to being pushed?"

Reese asked the question carefully, knowing how deep a wound she was feeling around.

Diane's eyes were full of tears. "Do you know what hurt most?" she asked. "Oh, I always said it was losing him. It was that Mary held me back and didn't let me go fight for him. But really, the thing that hurt most is that he was never Oneness. That I never got to know, with him, the depth of connection I know with Richard, or Mary, or even you. And I loved him. I still love him. More than anyone."

The office door opened to the sound of Susan just finishing up a call with someone, cheerful and friendly as ever. Diane hastily wiped her eyes, and Reese took a swallow of coffee. Her hands were shaking slightly. She didn't think it was the effect of the caffeine.

You didn't betray him, she wanted to tell Diane.

But Susan walked back into the kitchen, and she couldn't.

"We're in luck!" the housemother announced. "I just spoke with Dr. Smith, and he's going to come back to the house now to meet with you. All his appointments are for later, and he said he'd rather come see you than do paperwork at the moment." Her eyes sparkled. "I told him you were special."

Reese's mind went into an immediate attempt to interpret that. What exactly could this woman see? Did she know they were Oneness? Was this a trap?

Her heart was racing. Realizing that her hand was shaking even harder than before, she nevertheless raised the coffee to her lips and took another swallow. Easy, she told herself. Calm down.

Even if it was a trap, if Dr. Smith was coming back here empowered by the devil himself, Reese would be able to handle it. He was just one man, and she had faced demonic entities before. Alone, even.

And this time, she told herself as she glanced at Diane, she wasn't alone.

"That's wonderful," she heard Diane saying. Covering for her companion's sudden attack of panic. "We're really looking forward to meeting him."

Dr. Smith's office couldn't have been far away, because only ten minutes later—ten minutes mercifully filled by Susan's telling stories of children who had graduated from the home and gone into college and were doing well—Reese heard the hum of the double garage door again. Moments later a short, balding, energetic man with a warm smile and sparklingly intelligent eyes bounced into the house, across the floor, and into a double-handed, sincerely welcoming handshake.

Reese, on the other end of the handshake, had been prepared for anything but this.

"I'm Dr. Smith," he said. "Welcome, welcome. I'm so glad you're here." He greeted Diane just as warmly and then pulled up a stool at the counter beside them, angling himself so they could both see him. "Good day so far, Susan?" he asked.

"All except Alex," she said. "Nearly late for school and so much attitude again. Has he told you yet where he went last week?"

"Afraid not," Dr. Smith said. He sighed, a particular fussy kind of sigh given by someone trying to work out a problem but without success. "You're doing well, Susan. Just keep an eye on

     Rachel Starr Thomson

things. Let me know if he seems to be affecting anyone else. I want to give him time, but I don't want his attitude spreading—and I really don't want any of the other kids sneaking out. He won't tell me where he goes, but I have a bad feeling about it."

Reese listened to the exchange with interest. She was watching Dr. Smith as closely as she could without drawing attention to herself, but she couldn't see any sign of a demonic presence about him at all. He fit this place. In fact, his spirit was likely the heart of this place. Warm, open, wise.

"So, these ladies had a question for you," Susan said, sounding pleased and proud. "They want to know . . ."

"Well, now, let them ask it," Dr. Smith said, his eyes still smiling with good humour.

"I wanted to know," Reese said, "if you had to sum up your mission here in one word, what it would be?"

The smile vanished from his eyes, replaced by a serious-mindedness that was every bit as attractive as the smile.

"Freedom," he said firmly. "Our one goal here is freedom. Let me explain. Many people, if they came here and saw how we structure the young people's lives and how we keep them accountable and push them personally and academically, they would say we're all about discipline, or law. But we're not. What we're about is giving them the self-control, the self-discipline, they need to learn how to handle and make the most of freedom. Freedom without control is just anarchy. Those who want it come under the control of someone or something else—it's the great irony. You pursue freedom, wholeheartedly and without any ability to discipline yourself, and you end up enslaved to addictions, or the abuse of other people who are stronger than you, or just the drives and whims of your own body. It's the fastest way to total imprisonment, total bondage. But if you have the tools to control yourself, and the ability to think long-term and to set goals and walk with vision, not just drive, then you'll not just find freedom, but you'll know how to use it."

He sat back in his chair, the smile back in his eyes. "You know, that's what good parents, good homes, do for their kids. They raise them within certain parameters and help them discover themselves, and they equip them for life. The kids who come here have never had that, for the most part. They know they want to be free, but they're living with all these fears and insecurities and habits that will just kill them down the road—literally or figuratively. My whole goal is to take every one of these young people and equip them to walk free."

"I can only applaud that," Reese said.

"Do you . . . " she framed the question carefully. "Do you ever come out to the fishing village on the bay, about an hour west of here?"

He frowned. "No, can't say I know where that is. Why do you ask?"

Reese bowed her head for a moment, then looked him straight in the eyes. "Are you in trouble?"

The question seemed to take him totally aback. "Why . . . I don't know what you mean. Why do you ask that?"

"Legal trouble, anything? Under attack in any way?" She knew she was ignoring his question, but she was fixed. "Anything attached to that boy? Alex?"

Dr. Smith, in such fine form a minute ago, was clearly off

his guard now. He spluttered and shook his head, and Reese stood. "May I use your phone?"

He recovered himself enough to say, "Of course. Just down the hall there, in the office. Dial 9 to get out."

Reese nodded and headed to the office at a near jog, aware that Diane was glaring at her and that she was leaving all three of them totally confused.

Her hands were still shaking as she dialed the cell house, but for a different reason now. "Mary, hi. Can you put April on the phone? Thanks."

She waited a moment until April picked up. "Just quickly, describe the man who came to get Nick. The one whose name was Vincent Smith."

It only took a few seconds. "Thank you," Reese said. "I'll explain when I get home. Tell Richard and Mary to pray. Something . . . I have a bad feeling. We found something. But I'm not sure what yet."

She hung up and went back to the kitchen. The other three were waiting, apparently not having bothered to converse. She couldn't blame them. It wasn't like she'd left Diane much to work with.

"Someone is impersonating you," Reese said. "At least, someone has. I live in a . . . . a commune, sort of. A few days ago we took in a boy from a troubled neighbourhood after someone calling himself Dr. Vincent Smith tried to bully him away from his mother to come to his children's home. But he wasn't you. You don't match the description—any of the description. I just wondered if you might know who he was or why someone might be using your name."

Hive

"I have no idea," Dr. Smith said, clearly trying to process too much at once. "I've never heard of anyone doing this before. You're sure?"

"I'm sure," Reese said.

"This home has a good name among those who know about it, although we are a private organization and rather selectively connected," Dr. Smith said. "Someone might have been trying to use our reputation to get a foot in, though it seems they would be better served using a better-known name. But what . . . why . . ."

"The boy is special," Reese said. "I know, all children are special, but this one . . ."

She stopped.

What in the world was she supposed to say?

That one of her sisters in the Oneness had painted this boy in a mural, and that meant he was significant and powerful and played some role in an unfolding spiritual war?

Susan's shaky voice cut in. "Are you detectives?" she asked.

Reese's expression softened, and she turned toward the woman. "No," she said. "Not exactly. But we are trying to track down the imposter and find out why he wanted this boy. We'll take it to the police once we have something to go on."

"Impersonation is something to go on," Dr. Smith said. "And attempted abduction, from what you described. Personally, I'd be much happier if they were involved."

Reese nodded. "You're right. We'll call them and report what we know. Unfortunately that isn't much—but we have a description of the man and can tell them that he gave a false name. I'm sorry to have misled you about why we were here," Reese said, directing her apology at Susan. "You're not what we thought we'd find. For what it's worth, this place is remarkable."

"And so are you," Diane said, squeezing Susan's hand again and standing. "I'm guessing from Reese's tone that we need to leave?"

"I think so, yes," Reese said. "I'm sorry . . . I just need to follow something else up, and I'm afraid we may lose our window."

Dr. Smith reached into his coat pocket and pulled out a business card, which he handed to Reese. "Consider us friends, please," he said. "I would love to be kept posted on what you find out."

Reese took the card with a smile. "As much as I can," she said. "And the same goes for you. If we can do anything to help you—if any trouble comes up—"

Diane had already written the cell house number on the back of another business card before Reese could pull her thoughts together. "Just call," she said, handing it to Dr. Smith.

"Thank you," he said. "I may just do that."

Reese paused as they turned to go. "About Alex . . ." she said. "Keep a careful eye on him. I know you're already watching, but watch even closer. I don't think he's safe."

She didn't bother to explain. Halfway across the street to the car, Diane commented, "Well, that was an enigmatic closing."

"He's possessed," Reese said. "I saw it on his way out. I know they don't know what we are, but I hope they'll take my warning seriously."

Diane stopped. "Wait, what are you saying?"

"I think we did find the hive," Reese replied. "Or at least one of its offshoots."

She got into the car, and Diane slid in beside her. "Explain what you mean."

"A hive is a collective of possessed human beings," Reese said. "It usually lives together, at least at first. A hive can look frighteningly like a Oneness cell, and even claim good reasons for its existence, but the heart is different—totally, completely different. Where his goal for those kids"—she nodded toward the house—"is freedom, a hive's goal is to enslave. But it won't stay centralized in one place. It will send out feelers. Possession often spreads from one person to another. Not exactly like a disease, because every person has to open the door to it individually, but by using human agency to convince others to open those doors. That children's home is a target. The hive wants to spread from Alex to the other kids."

She grimaced. "I think Dr. Smith is a good foil. His wife and Susan too. They really love those kids, and that will make it hard for the hive to spread. But it's going to try. The impersonation has something to do with that—the fake wasn't just trying to ride on the home's reputation. He's trying to bring the real Dr. Smith down somehow."

Diane gave that a moment of thought as they sped off, too fast for the residential neighbourhood.

"Almost anything could have happened to Nick," she said. "And his mother would have told police it was Dr. Smith who took him."

"Which, if it didn't lead to prison, would at least lead to

     Rachel Starr Thomson

slander and a legal battle," Reese finished. "And if it was all horrific and traumatic enough, it could turn even someone like Vincent Smith into a different man. Maybe a man who can be seduced into a hive himself."

Diane thought about that for another moment.

"Where are we going?" she asked.

"School," Reese answered. "We're going to follow Alex."

* * * * *

Tyler woke up when the sun came streaming through his window with a force far too great for early morning.

He had not prayed the night before. He had fallen asleep.

He realized this with a surprising sense of disappointment in himself. And frustration. Because he knew that as Oneness, he had a job to do in the world. Something about serving it and holding it together. And he didn't even know how to do the most basic part of that.

A lot of good he was.

"Care to say what's eating you?" Chris asked.

Tyler jumped. He hadn't noticed Chris standing in his doorway, leaning on his noncasted shoulder.

"I can't pray," Tyler said. "The most basic job of the Oneness, and I can't do it. I'm just feeling a little useless is all."

"You're wrong," Chris said, looking behind as if to ascertain the hallway was all clear. As apparently it was. "Praying is not the most basic job of the Oneness."

"What is?" Tyler asked, irked that Chris was pretending to know more than he did.

"Love," Chris answered.

Ouch. Maybe he did know more.

"Why are you here?" Tyler asked. "I was sleeping."

"It's the crack of ten," Chris answered. "And if you keep sleeping, they aren't going to believe we're well enough to leave. I came to rouse you and tell you to act like a man and come eat a man's breakfast. I don't know about you, but I am ready to get out of here."

"Coming," Tyler said, groaning as he pushed himself up. There was something about last night . . . something other than his failure to pray. Something he'd wanted to tell Chris. What was it?

The memories came back to his groggy mind. Rick. The hitchhiker.

The hitchhiker.

The hitchhiker with freaky black eyes.

Tyler half-leaped from the bed and nearly stumbled over his own feet. Chris was already out of the room and halfway down the hall.

"Chris, wait," he called as he pulled on the khakis he'd been given yesterday. "Hold up a minute."

Chris reappeared. "What?"

Tyler hesitated. "Why are you up so late?"

"Slept like a log. I tried to wake up earlier but couldn't."

"Couldn't?"

"I don't know what they're giving us, but they're drugging us all up a lot more than I like."

"Listen, Chris, I talked to the truck driver last night. He woke up. Ran out of pain meds."

Chris raised an eyebrow. "Oh yeah?"

"Yes, and he said"—Tyler finished pulling on a shirt and headed for the door—"he said he can't remember anything about the wreck, but he had picked up a hitchhiker and they were talking. And then he blanked out or something, because he can't remember anything else. But he said the hitchhiker was a college kid with freaky black eyes."

He stopped triumphantly.

"The Wizard," Chris said.

"That's my guess."

Chris whistled. "So that accident wasn't an accident."

"Not that I'm an expert in the demonic, but I wouldn't think so."

"Which means," Chris said slowly, "that maybe something wants us to be here."

Tyler hesitated, his triumph needled by conscience and concern for these people. Chris was already antagonistic toward them, but Tyler still wasn't convinced he knew enough about them. They said they were Oneness. They cared about each other and took in strangers. They weren't demonic as far as he could tell.

But shoot, he couldn't even manage to pray. How was he supposed to tell something like that?

"Maybe," he agreed slowly. "But I don't think that necessarily means these people are in on it, if you know what I mean. Just because demons are pulling strings doesn't mean everybody's a puppet."

Chris gave him a look and disappeared back into the hallway. Food smells greeted them as soon as they pushed their way out of the storeroom at the bottom of the stairs—bread, tomatoes, something else. Not breakfast food. Everyone in the community, Tyler suspected, got up and ate way before the crack of ten.

When they stepped into the kitchen, no one would meet their eyes. Julie was there, and the other younger women from yesterday, but they kept their expressions downcast. Every movement spoke nerves and unhappiness.

Lorrie appeared in the doorway. Her expression alone was unveiled—and hostile. She folded her arms and nodded.

"You'll wait in the dining room," she said. "Jacob will be in to speak with you in a minute."

"Have we done something?" Chris asked, belligerent.

Lorrie's eyes fixed on a surprised Tyler. "Why don't you ask your friend here?" She gestured to the dining room.

Tyler and Chris exchanged glances.

"Let's go," Chris grumbled. "I think I'd welcome the chance to have a little heart-to-heart with the kingpin."

Trying to ignore the miserable, sinking feeling in his stomach, Tyler followed Chris to the dining room to wait.

 Rachel Starr Thomson

Reese and Diane pulled up outside the schoolyard and sat in the morning air for a few minutes, their windows rolled down so they could see clearly and the shouts of children playing on the yard of the elementary school right next door carried over. They had the car angled so they could see the big double red doors at the front of the high school.

"I wish I had a way in there," Reese said. "He might not come out."

"I'm not sure I really understand what we're doing here," Diane said.

"If I'm right, and Alex is part of a hive, then he's not working alone. Most likely his other contacts are here—at school. Or else he's sneaking off during school to meet with them."

"Dr. Smith said he had gone out at night."

"Yes, but just once or twice. That's not regular enough. Either he's getting contact from other students or he's playing hooky."

"So you hope he's playing hooky," Diane finished. "So you can follow him."

"We. Yes."

"He's not going to come out the front doors," Diane pointed out.

"I'm not exactly looking for him."

"What are you looking for?"

"Demons."

Diane cleared her throat. "Invisible demons?"

"I've been tracking this hive a long time," Reese said. "And I am very, very familiar with how it feels. I can usually sense them."

"Is that why you're so convinced this kid is part of the hive and not just an individual case? Because he felt familiar?"

"Actually, no," Reese said. She gave a tight smile. "Because he recognized me."

She leaned back against her seat and sighed. The shouts and laughter of children at the elementary school were growing louder, like the longer they played the more wild and enthusiastic they got. Oh, the tenuous joy of recess.

Their earlier conversation came back to mind.

"You didn't betray him," Reese said.

"What?"

"Douglas."

Diane kept her face forward, staring toward the high school doors.

Reese kept going. "That you wanted it for him so badly only

shows how much you loved him."

"I don't want to talk about it," Diane said.

Reese closed her mouth and sat back again.

Compared to the wild and rambunctious playground next door, the high school seemed dark and imposing. And utterly still.

"Why now?" Diane asked after a few more minutes of waiting. "We could have stayed at the home and talked until he came back from school. I don't think they would have kicked us out. At least, not until you got so intense on them."

"He saw me on his way out," Reese said. "And whatever's living in him knew me. He was terrified. I think they'll try something today if they can. At the very least they'll try contact, and Alex will lead us to the rest of them."

"And then we'll die," Diane said. "Because we'll find ourselves in the middle of some horde, alone and totally outnumbered."

"We're not alone," Reese said. She grinned. "And we don't always die when we're totally outnumbered."

A flicker of movement at the side of the school caught Reese's eye—and she was out of the car and running before Diane could move or think. With a shout forming in her throat, the older woman opened her door and tried to rush out. Reese was already across the street and over the fence. A long, black sword had formed in her hand. She was running, another, skinnier figure was running a ways ahead of her, feet pounding pavement—and then Reese caught up and drove her sword right through the back of a teenage boy in black who screamed and dropped to the ground.

Diane, stuck at trying to clamber over the fence, stopped and gaped. The shout died in her throat.

What had Reese just done?

The boy was writhing on the ground. Reese was crouched beside him, her hands on his shoulders, holding him down. The sword was nowhere to be seen.

Diane was out of breath when she caught up. The boy glared up at her with a look so hateful it stopped her in her tracks.

"Reese . . ."

"Help me," Reese got out.

Diane just stood there, lost. When had she seen this last? A teenager . . . the black clothes . . . the hatred. All that was missing was the wild, drug-high eyes, the insanity of the boys who came and killed her husband.

She let out a wail and sank to her knees.

"Take his feet!" Reese gasped. "Help me calm him down!"

The boy's feet were thrashing. Somewhere, Diane found the inner strength to grab them and hold them. The boy's body kept twisting, jerking, but it lacked strength.

"It's not gone," Reese said, willing Diane to get it, to understand. "It's holding on too tight. He doesn't want it to go, so it's still in there. But I wounded it. We have a few minutes."

Reese got out of her crouch onto her knees and leaned over the boy's face, arresting his twisting head with her eyes. "Hold still," she commanded. "I want to talk to you. Listen to me."

"Who?" the boy spat. "Who do you want?"

"Alex," Reese said quietly, but firm. "I want Alex. Let him talk."

For a moment the boy's eyes clouded over, and then someone was there—insolent, angry, but more scared than before. Younger. Human.

"Freak," he said. "Let me go."

"Tell me what happened to you," Reese said. "I want to help. I can help. Talk to me."

The skinny face grimaced, but the eyes were still angry. "I don't want to tell you nothing."

"Do you want to be free?" Reese asked, quiet, insistent. "Really free?"

"You been talking to Dr. Smith? I will be free, soon as I get the hell away from him. And people like you."

"That's a lie," Reese said. "You're already enslaved to something else. You know that. They may tell you they're giving you power, but they're not. They're making you a slave. You can get free from them, Alex. We can help you."

The eyes reclouded, and the expression changed again. Its fear, and its youth, was gone. Otherwise it was nearly identical.

"He doesn't want your help," the demon said.

And it was true.

Suddenly Reese's sword was back in her hand, and she held the tip of it to the boy's chest. He ceased twisting and trying to get away, instead lying horribly still on the pavement.

Diane closed her eyes. Not looking. Or she might have been praying that no one else would see either.

"Do you want to keep playing this game?" Reese asked.

"You won't keep hurting the boy."

"It doesn't hurt him as bad as it hurts you. You, I can maybe drive right out."

"You can't. I won't go."

Reese shrugged. "Your decision."

She raised the tip to strike down.

"Stop!" the boy's voice screamed out. "Don't!"

"Then tell me something," Reese answered. Sweat was pouring down her face. "Tell me where to find the rest of you. You're branching out. Where's the hub?"

"You're the one who attacked the core," the demon said. "We almost killed you."

"I think I gave as good as I got."

"But you didn't win. You can't win."

Reese pressed the sword down. The boy screamed.

Diane let go of his feet and was at Reese's side, hand on her arm. "Reese," she said calmly, "let him go."

"I'm cornering a demon," Reese said through gritted teeth.

"I know, but it's in a boy. You're going to do damage. Let him go."

Reese looked up and met Diane's eyes. Her own were full of pain, full of anger. Diane was calm.

Sucking in a breath of air, Reese let go of the hilt. Her sword evaporated.

 Rachel Starr Thomson

She still held the boy's shoulders. He was quivering, but no longer twisting and struggling to get away. His eyes were still the demon's eyes, laughing and taunting. But the body was the boy's.

"Hey!" Reese heard a shout from across the yard. "What's going on over there?"

She glanced up. A teacher. "Diane," she said. "Please. A seizure. Tell them the boy had a seizure. It's true."

Diane nodded and stood, walking calmly toward the teacher. Reese looked back down at the boy, at Alex, for what she knew was the last minute with him.

"Please tell me something," she whispered. "Alex. Tell me something."

"They're going to get your friend," the teen whispered. "They're trying to get him."

"Who? What friend?"

"Her son." He closed his eyes. "They already got him at the warehouse."

Diane and the teacher were drawing closer. She was trying to stall him, but she couldn't do so beyond reason.

"Alex," Reese said, more urgently now, "I can drive it out. But you have to want to be free. You have to choose it. Just tell me that you're choosing it, and I'll help you."

He kept his eyes closed and shook his head.

The teacher was there, kneeling over Alex and trying to lift his head.

"We saw him from across the street," Reese said, slowly withdrawing, slowly standing. "We tried to help."

"Thank you," the teacher said. "We'll call an ambulance."

Reese nodded. "I think he's out of danger."

"Still, we need to get him checked out."

Check away, Reese thought. You're not going to find the real problem.

She had known what she was facing, and even she hadn't found the real problem.

Other school authorities were arriving. They surrounded Alex and talked to him, but he didn't respond. Reluctant, she and Diane walked away.

They got back into the car without saying a word.

And just sat there.

"You said yourself, Reese," Diane said finally. "He has to choose it for himself."

"I thought we could at least force something out of the demon. They're cowards. Not hard to break, usually."

"Maybe it's more scared of something else than it is of you."

"Likely," Reese conceded. "In a hive they have to work together more than usual; there are power structures and things."

"And power structures don't like to be betrayed," Diane said.

Reese lowered her voice. "He did tell me one thing." She swallowed. "They're going after Chris. They already have somehow."

Diane's whole body tensed, electrified. "What? They can't have! I would know."

"Chris isn't Oneness," Reese said quietly. "The connection

isn't there; something could have happened and you wouldn't feel it."

"He's my son," Diane insisted. "I felt what happened to Douglas; I feel what happens to Chris. Oneness isn't the only strong tie in this world."

Reese took the rebuke. And added, "And we would know if something happened to Tyler. As long as they're together . . ."

"I'm sure they are," Diane said.

And Reese knew that surety, that confidence, was as much a bluffing, determined kind of hope as it was any real knowledge. But she let it go. Better to think that they were together, and so Chris was connected to the Oneness and they would know if something really bad happened to him.

But this at least confirmed one thing: their disappearance wasn't just random, and they hadn't just gone on vacation and forgotten to tell anyone.

"Alex . . . I think it was Alex talking to me, not the demon . . . said something about Chris and the warehouse. But I'm not sure what he meant. The core isn't there anymore."

"They would have gone there, though," Diane said. "If Chris came into town because he wanted to find the hive, which I think he did, they would have gone back there because it's the last link."

"But there's no reason to go back there," Reese argued. "They cleared out."

"Just because a hope is futile doesn't mean you're not going to follow it up," Diane said. "It's been driving him crazy, doing nothing."

Because of Reese, they both knew but didn't say. As long as the hive was out there, Reese was both in danger and unavenged, as far as Chris was concerned, and all of her grief and pain didn't have a reason, a victory attached to it. He'd been going nuts trying to make the world right for her.

Not an easy task, making the world right. The Oneness had been trying to do it for centuries.

"I just wish we'd learned something more concrete," Reese said, leaning her head forward and resting it on the steering wheel. "We can go back to the warehouse."

"Hmm," Diane said.

"What?"

"You said you wanted a way into the school, right?"

"Yes," Reese said. "But I'm afraid this is as close as we're going to get."

"Do Oneness kids go to school?"

"Sometimes," Reese said. "Why?"

"How old are those twins?"

"Tony and Angelica? Too old. I don't know. Maybe eighteen."

"So maybe not too old," Diane countered. "Especially if one of them needed remedial schooling."

Reese's eyes lit slowly. "Wait. Maybe you're right." The thought of either of the twins playing undercover student made her want to laugh, even in the midst of so much awfulness. She had a feeling they'd be more than the school bargained for. All she would need was to find them an address in Brass so they

   Rachel Starr Thomson

could attend the school.

"Better yet," she said slowly, "why don't we put them into the children's home?"

"Say what?"

"That home is in danger . . . serious danger. And the twins would need an address in Brass to be able to attend the school. If we can convince Dr. Smith to take them in, they can go undercover at the school, and watch out for the children's home, and keep a close eye on Alex. Maybe even help him. It's perfect."

"What if Alex's . . . demon . . . recognizes the twins like it did you?"

"Then some of the plans won't work. But they can still protect the home and maybe get through to Alex somehow. Either way it's a step in the right direction."

Reese took a right, headed for Lincoln and the cell house there. She hadn't planned that, but it seemed a better idea than going to the warehouse.

Or maybe, despite her ardent protestations that the demonic core had cleared out, she was still too afraid of that place.

"Speaking of Alex and steps in the right direction," Diane said, "is there a reason you abandoned your first plan? Follow Alex and hope he leads us to others?"

"I don't know. No. I saw him and changed my mind."

They drove on and crossed a highway, taking the rural route to the city.

"Are you okay, Reese? I know things have changed for the better, but . . ."

Reese cut her off. "If you're asking whether I can control myself enough to be on a mission like this, the answer is yes."

Diane was silent for a minute. Then she said, "Actually, I just wanted to know if you were okay."

Reese's eyes filled with tears. "I lost so much. I'm trying to come back."

"But you're not back yet."

"No."

Diane looked out the window. "Sometimes things take time."

"Why did you stop me back there?" Reese asked, choking down something in her throat.

"Because of a memory. I remembered myself when Douglas was killed and Mary held me back. I never realized before she didn't do that just for me. She was trying to protect those kids. They were just kids, you know, the murderers. I think Mary hoped they could be helped somehow, in time to prevent the tragedy. That her brother could deliver them of the demons or Douglas could stop their attack. And she thought I would get in the way and maybe do something awful, and then I would be guilty for the rest of my life for killing children."

She paused.

"Maybe she was right."

"Thank you," Reese said quietly. "You were right. I would have done damage."

"You're welcome." It was awkward, stilted.

"I'm not sure what happened to me back there."

    Rachel Starr Thomson

"When you really go through something," Diane said slowly, "it can get into you, and it turns into this thing that moves you sometimes, makes decisions for you, and you don't even know why."

Reese smiled and nodded, sadly.

"You know, that's one reason I was so angry with the Oneness for so many years," Diane went on. "I thought, when I became Oneness, that kind of thing couldn't happen to me anymore. But it did."

"We aren't perfect," Reese said. "The only difference between the Oneness and everyone else is we're tapped into something beyond ourselves for strength. We don't think we can be human all on our own."

"You're right."

"We."

Diane smiled back. "We're right, then."

Two hours, a visit, and a phone call later, and they were back in the office at Dr. Smith's children's home, with the door shut and Dr. Smith regarding them with a seriousness almost displaced by scepticism. The twins sat alongside Reese and Diane, both looking like they were itching for some kind of action.

What action they expected in a psychologist's office was anyone's guess.

"I know you believe in the soul, Dr. Smith" Reese was saying. "That's what you study. and you're good and wise about that. But do you believe in the supernatural? In the spirit world?"

"I've reserved judgment," Dr. Smith said, still eyeing them all with suspicion.

"Well, if we're not asking you to completely give up reserving it, I guess we're asking that you play along for a little while. What we saw in Alex's eyes wasn't just mental illness. And we have dealt with it before. I believe you're a target, sir, and the danger is not small. We can help."

He cleared his throat. "I just don't know. Demons—I like you, miss, but with all respect, you haven't been completely upfront with me from the beginning. This morning when you first arrived you were just potential donors—"

"In our defence, we didn't say that. Susan assumed it. I just asked to see the home."

"Very well. But you took some time to set her straight."

"Until I met you, I didn't know for certain that you weren't a man who tried to bully a boy away from his mother, and not exactly through the usual channels. Can you blame us for being careful?"

"I suppose not." He eyed the twins again. "They're a little old."

"Surely you've had eighteen-year-olds here before."

"Not on this kind of short notice. And we're nearly full."

"Which means you do have a little room." Reese spread her hands. "Please, sir, just give us a chance. If the costs are an issue, we'll find a way to pay their room and board."

They had debated, on the way here, whether to be upfront with the good doctor or try to convince him that the twins were actually in need of a home—and were a year or two younger than they actually were to boot. They'd decided in favour of truth.

The Spirit, in which they dwelt, seemed to favour truth. Lies

     Rachel Starr Thomson

were characteristic of the enemy. Which didn't make them seem less attractive in a case like this—but prior experience won out, and they opted to be honest.

Diane had been dubious of the plan and looked more unimpressed with it by the minute.

To all their surprise, it was Tony who broke the stalemate.

"Sir, you've been dealing with this Alex kid for a while, right?"

Dr. Smith assented.

"And you've probably seen some kids like him before?"

Yes.

"And I'm guessing that you have lots of science and formulas and things for everybody, and every condition, and that these kids don't always fit those. Because you're dealing with something beyond that, and you don't know what."

He smiled, a small smile that spoke worlds about how much headway Tony was making. Reese marveled at the man's open soul. There was no pride here preventing him from being convinced: if someone could show him that he was wrong, he would not only acquiesce but smile while doing it.

"That's all true," he said.

"Well, that's what we want to help you with. That something beyond. And maybe we can show you some things that will help you with other kids too."

Dr. Smith stood. "You win," he said. He fixed them all with a stern look—genuinely stern. "You two will agree to abide by all house rules at all times. If you feel it's necessary to do something outside the rules because of this mission of yours, you will discuss it with me or my wife first—I will be sharing all this with her, so she'll know everything I do. And you all will put the safety and well-being of the other young people here first. That includes Alex. And 'well-being' doesn't just mean that I don't want you to get anyone physically hurt or killed. I am doing everything I can to give everyone here a leg up in life. I don't want anything interfering with that. Many of these kids are still fragile. Do you understand?"

"Yes sir," everyone but Diane said in unison. She nodded.

"This is not just talk. If you do not do what I'm asking, I will pack both of you out of here, and I will call the police on all of you."

Reese stood and held out her hand. "We are fully in agreement," she said. "The kids matter to us too. As do you. This is a special place. We only want to protect it."

The sternness left his face, and he shook her hand. "I hope that's true. Against much of my better judgment, I like you and am inclined to trust you. But I wanted to make the terms clear."

"As you have." Diane and the twins stood as well, and each shook the doctor's hand.

"How long until you two can move in?" he asked.

Tony grinned. "Our bags are in the car. We're ready. Oh . . . and when's our first day of school?"

* * * * *

     Rachel Starr Thomson

Chris and Tyler sat waiting at the long kitchen table, dwarfed by its size and totally unattended, for close to twenty minutes. Chris was getting twitchy, and angrier by the minute; Tyler just felt confused. The contrast to the days before couldn't have been stronger: there was no tending now, no soup, no smiling, laughing women. The only thing that was the same was their awareness that they were being watched.

Clearly they were in trouble, but why?

Lorrie had intimated it was Tyler's fault somehow. But what in the world? He hadn't done anything but talk to Rick Brodie in the middle of the night, and that only because the man was obviously in pain and had woken him up with his groaning.

Anyway, talking to someone wasn't a sin. This was a free country.

Though maybe not, he had to concede, a free community.

When Jacob finally entered, looking larger than normal, carefully groomed, and horribly stern, Chris looked as though he could hardly stop himself from jumping up and punching the man in the face.

But Tyler shrank. Jacob's marked charisma, his powers of leadership and inspiration, were all turned against him now, and he felt like something lower than a rat and more despised than the mat at the door of a mudroom. He was stricken by the awful feeling of having betrayed someone.

But what in the world had he done?

Jacob stood for a few minutes, glowering down, during which neither of the boys rose. Chris sullenly met the man's gaze; Tyler shrunk away from it.

Finally he sat and laid his hands on the table. "You should count yourselves lucky I didn't throw you out," Jacob opened the conversation.

"I think in this country people are presumed innocent until proven guilty, and are usually charged with a crime. Would you care to tell us why we are out of favour?" Chris tossed the answer in Jacob's face, and the man went dark.

Anger.

Tyler had found himself comparing this man to Richard now and again, but he had never seen an expression like that on Richard's face.

"Maybe you don't know," Jacob said. "Though I will hold you guilty by association. If I'd had to pick one of you to finger as trouble, it would have been you. You," he nodded at Tyler, "I had hopes for."

Tyler squeaked out something in response. Jacob's anger only burned harder.

"Where were you at midnight last night?" he demanded.

"Probably in Rick Brodie's room," Tyler said. "The driver. I heard him groaning and went to check on him."

Why did he feel like he was confessing a sin?

The admission didn't appear to do anything to alleviate Jacob's wrath. "Where else?" he asked.

"In my room."

"Where else?"

Tyler's mouth opened, but for the life of him he didn't know what was supposed to come out of it. Jacob stood and began to pace. "I have done everything I can do to separate this community from the world and keep them safe. We block media, we're careful about who we allow in here. You've seen the results: ours is a happy, peaceful, innocent family."

"Don't tell me he was meeting with a girl," Chris mumbled.

The revelation was instant. "Oh," Tyler blurted before he could stop himself, "Miranda . . ."

"Glad you remember," Jacob said. He was seething. The anger was real.

Tyler felt himself, deep down, beginning to tremble. He'd felt sick since being called in here, and Jacob's anger was blinding, like getting hit with unexpected punch after punch, but this was confusion, and he was starting to sense that the trouble was deeper than he'd realized.

"We did right by you," Jacob said through clenched teeth. "We took you in and helped you and nursed you back to health faster than any hospital could have. We even made a police report, and you can guess how much we love involving the law in anything."

He shot Chris a look. "Not because we're doing anything illegal. Because the world does not understand our ways, and they are of the world."

"I think they might consider holding three people against their will illegal," Chris said. His own anger was starting to rise, to show up in his eyes with frightening clarity—not now the annoyance and resentment at being treated like children and intimidated, but the anger of witnessing a friend threatened and wrongfully accused.

"You weren't here against your wills."

"We were drugged, and denied real access to a phone—I don't know what you did, but I'm sure the problem with getting through wasn't with the other end—and never asked whether we wanted to leave or given an offer of transportation."

The man's expression grew slightly sullen. "We're not under obligation to offer you anything."

"And you call yourselves Oneness," Chris spat. "You're no more Oneness than I am. Less, maybe. They would have helped, not imprisoned. What about that man upstairs? Has he even been awake enough to tell you what he wants, or how to contact his family, other than last night?"

"Chris," Tyler whispered.

Chris ignored him. "And what about your own people? Are they all here because they want to be? You're threatening us and acting like Tyler molested someone, and if I know him all he did was trip over the kid in the hallway."

"We have chosen to be—"

"I'm not done!" Chris roared. He was standing now, chest to chest with Jacob, and Tyler had never realized how big his friend was, or how truly intimidating, even with his arm in a cast. "You do a bunch of good things and you want to point to them and tell us to overlook all the bad things, all the signals that something is really wrong around here, but you know what? That kind of good thing is just a lie. And I don't ignore signals."

"Chris," Tyler pressed. Chris still ignored him.

"So we are leaving," Chris said, "before you can get a chance to spew your venom about what you think Tyler was doing last

      Rachel Starr Thomson

night. I don't even want to hear it, do you understand me? I have no tolerance for lies, and I can see in your face that you have nothing else to say. Now show me the way out of here, and either offer me a ride or I will walk."

"You're fifty miles from civilization."

"I don't care."

Man to man, they stood and faced each other down. And Tyler's mouth went dry.

Behind Jacob, someone had moved into the door frame.

The Wizard.

Chris went ballistic when he saw him. Something distracted him from the stare-down with Jacob, and he looked just enough to the man's left to see the college kid standing in the doorway. Chris shouted and flew at him, broken arm and all. And what happened Tyler couldn't actually see, but Chris went sprawling and landed at the kid's feet.

Dead, Tyler thought for one terrifying second.

No, just unconscious.

He rebuked his own panic and stupidity.

And slowness, because he was also unconscious before he could think anything else, and when he woke up he was looking into the Wizard's demonic eyes.

He had no idea where he was.

Nor did he seem to have much control over his mouth.

"You're the hitchhiker," he garbled.

"And you're Oneness," the Wizard said.

"What's your name?"

The Wizard smiled. "Which one of us?"

Tyler grimaced. "Never mind."

His brain was struggling to interpret his surroundings. Walls and dark and it seemed like everything was rocking, and there was noise . . .

"Where are we?"

"In the back of a truck, actually."

"Why?"

"We're going where you wanted to go. To find the hive."

"Where's Chris?" The mention of the hive brought a lot of things rushing back, and Tyler struggled to sit up. He realized he was lying on a hard surface, his limbs heavier than they'd ever been, his face flat against the floor and turned toward the Wizard.

Who was sitting.

"Oh, he's here. We don't want him to miss anything."

"Like what?"

"Like when we kill you." The Wizard smiled as though this was a pleasant announcement.

Oh.

"Which is scheduled to happen . . ."

"Soon, soon."

Tyler tried to move but couldn't. He didn't think he was

bound, although his sense of his own body was so vague and oppressed that he couldn't be sure. He was essentially paralyzed, whether by drugs or by something more spiritual he didn't know.

But he wanted to know. He wanted to know so many things.

It was fairly clear to him that he wasn't going to make it out of this one. If the others were here, if they could stand united, if he had more experience in the Spirit—sword-wielding, even praying—maybe he would stand a chance. But he was alone, he couldn't move, and he had absolutely no idea what to do. To his surprise he felt little emotion about this—maybe it was the drugs. No fear really, or sorrow. But he did want to know.

He wanted all this to make sense.

"You're possessed," he said.

"Yes."

"Who am I talking to, anyway?"

"Doesn't matter. Even we're not really sure."

"Right." He struggled to put his thoughts together. "You were with a Oneness cell. Why . . ."

The Wizard laughed. "They are hardly Oneness."

"But they are. Jacob is. I felt it. I was trying to tell Chris. I wondered all that time, but I finally knew for sure . . ."

He was babbling and he knew it, but he didn't really care. Saying it all out loud meant he could think about it, could process it.

The Wizard laughed again. "Yes, Jacob is. And he is convinced he is the only real manifestation of Oneness in the world today. But his community is no cell. Surely you felt that. Jacob does not bring others into the Oneness. He brings others under his own control."

"But why?"

The Wizard's eyes were dancing. "If he brought people into the Spirit, he could not control them. He would lose them. He does not want to lose anyone."

"But why were you there?"

"Because Jacob has gone blind in his fear and his need to dominate. He invites us in. He only knows that we are power, and power is what he thinks the Spirit is. So he believes we are of God."

Tyler closed his eyes.

"Are you lying to me?" he asked.

"No."

"Don't you usually lie?"

"Yes. But not when the truth is enough to bring despair."

Despair.

He was supposed to feel despair.

He didn't.

His eyes still closed, keeping the Wizard out, Tyler tried to pray again. He still felt detached, curious. He wanted to know if it would work. If, this separated from everyone and everything, he was just as fully connected as ever.

He found, to his surprise, that he was.

How he entered into it this time he really didn't know, but as he reached out with his spirit he knew he was stepping into something wider, deeper, higher than himself. Something flow-ing and throbbing like blood, like a heartbeat; something full of life and stronger than the power—powers—gloating at him in this truck. The something whispered deep inside his soul, "All shall be well." And he believed it.

But at the same time, tapping into the Spirit broke his emotional numbness. Feeling swept into him, almost choked him: sorrow, immense and deep, sorrow for Jacob and for his community, sorrow at their fear and their blindness, sorrow at how much they had traded for how little.

The sorrow was wise and ancient, and when Tyler opened his eyes again he felt older, more mature, more capable.

And fear had come into the Wizard's eyes.

He almost laughed. Did it really take so little to shake them? Were the demons really so weak after all?

They were still probably going to kill him, but the fear in this kid's eyes and the peace filling Tyler's whole being told the real story.

He heard sirens.

"No," the Wizard said.

The fear was stronger.

The sirens grew louder, and the truck rocked; the driver was braking. They lurched into a slow-down and gravel crunched under the tires. The Wizard was on his feet, looking wildly around for some way to hide his prisoners and himself, but there was nothing.

And Tyler laughed. Someone had called the police after all.

The dead policemen made the news. Diane called and told Mary to turn it on, but as there was no television in the house, they ended up going to her place instead. The news was playing the report every fifteen minutes, so they caught it again.

Mary and Richard and Reese watched in silence; April had been left home with Nick. They didn't want him to see.

Mary looked sick as she turned away from the news report. All that showed on the camera was the highway, cordoned off, and a small swarm of emergency vehicles. But the reporter's face was as ashen as Mary's.

They were giving details as they got them. No names yet.

Reading between the lines, Mary guessed they hadn't been able to identify the bodies by sight.

The camera flashed a picture of the crumpled, overturned police car. It looked like it had been totalled by a cement truck.

The men had not died in the car.

There had been two of them, and the deaths were so horrific, so bloody and violent, that Richard switched the report off halfway through as yet another ream of details began to come out, horrifying but still, they guessed, being played down.

When it came to decency, even the media had limits.

They were all standing, crowded around the TV on Diane's kitchen counter. No one sat. No one moved.

The word "demon" didn't have to be spoken.

"Call the twins," Reese finally said. "Make sure they've heard." Then almost as an afterthought, "I'll do it."

"Where is my son?" Diane asked, hollow.

"He's still all right," Richard said. "We would know if something had happened to Tyler . . ."

"But Tyler isn't Chris."

"But they're together. I'm sure they're together."

Reese left.

When she stepped into the cell house, the phone was ringing. She wondered briefly where April was, but crossed the floor and answered the phone without bothering to find out.

"Hello?"

The voice on the other end was timid. A girl's voice, young.

Terrified.

"Hello, there . . . there's been a death."

Reese put out her hand to steady herself on the counter. "I know," she said. "We saw it on the news."

"On the news? How? Nobody knows yet . . . I just called

the police, and . . ."

"Wait, stop," Reese said. "It's okay. It's going to be all right. Who is this?"

The girl didn't answer the question. "How can it be on the—"

Reese stopped her. "Wait, it's okay. I think we're talking about different deaths. Can you tell me who you are? Why you're calling me?"

The girl was silent for a heartbeat. Then, "Chris gave me your number." Her voice got fainter. "Is this Reese?"

"Yes," Reese answered, her heart suddenly pounding. She couldn't stay on her feet—she slid down to the floor, wrapping the phone cord around her arm like she was afraid it would fly away. "Is Chris with you?" she asked, forcing her voice to stay steady.

"No, he's gone . . . they took them both away." The girl sounded like she wanted to cry. "I'm not supposed to know anything, but I can't help it. I just saw, and then . . ."

And then she was crying, and Reese's knuckles were going white around the phone. Her eyes cast around the kitchen. Where was April? Why weren't Richard and Mary back yet? She didn't know if she could handle this alone.

"Please," she said far, far more calmly and soothingly than she would have thought possible, "tell me who this is. I want to help you. I'll come help you. Just tell me."

"M-Miranda," the girl got out.

"Where are you, Miranda?"

"At home."

"Where do you live?"

"I don't know. In the country."

Reese closed her eyes. "What's your address, honey?"

"I don't know."

She opened her eyes again. Was the girl really ignorant of her own address, or just too scared to remember it?

"Do you know what road you live on?"

"Just our road. I don't think it has a name."

Reese decided to change tacks. "Can you tell me what happened?"

"I don't know! After they left, Jacob was so angry, and, and, we were just taking care of him . . . I don't know why he died."

"Jacob died?"

"No, the man who was here with Chris and Tyler. Rick Brodie."

Reese let out a breath she hadn't known she was holding. That was information they could find a way to use.

"Miranda, what's your full name?" she asked. "And Jacob's?"

"I'm Miranda Hopkins. Jacob is . . . I don't know. I've never heard his last name. He leads our community."

"Did you say you called the police?" Reese asked, quietly.

"Yes. I was scared. They weren't going to call. Jacob said it wasn't a good idea to let the world in. They were just going to bury him. But I'm scared."

"Why did Chris give you this number?"

"He said if I was ever scared, to call you. He said you would help me."

"I will," Reese promised. She didn't know, but she would. There had to be a way to trace this call—Richard would have the connections to do it.

"Are you calling from home?" she asked.

"Y-es."

"Miranda, listen, I'm going to come find you," Reese said. "Do you have someone you can trust? Anyone?"

"My mother."

The answer surprised Reese but made her glad. "Okay. Stick by her and wait for me. I don't know how long I'll be—maybe a couple of days. But I'll come as soon as I can."

She knew from the girl's voice that she needed her.

And she wasn't going to let Chris down for the world.

"I have to go," Miranda said. Her voice sounded more frightened again, and Reese thought she could make out faint background noise—nothing discernible.

"It's okay. You did the right thing by calling. I'm coming to help you."

There was a click.

Reese unwound the cord from around her arm and stared at the phone.

The front door banged.

"Richard?"

"Yes." He came into the kitchen. "What in the world are you doing?"

"Trouble just called," Reese said. "And her name is Miranda."

"What are you talking about?" He was on the floor, crouching beside her, serious as anything.

"Can we trace a call that just came in?"

"Yeah, we can do that."

"Then let's," Reese said. "Quickly. I just got a call from a girl in trouble—Chris gave her this number. But she couldn't give me an address. Either she doesn't know where she lives, or she just couldn't remember it. I think the first. Wherever it is, Chris and Tyler were just there."

"Were?"

"She said someone took them away. She sounds terrified." Reese sighed. "And someone else is dead. She gave me a name: Rick Brodie."

"It's something to go on," Richard said.

Reese closed her eyes and leaned her head against the side of the counter. In a moment she would find fight, drive, energy.

In this moment, all she wanted to do was let the world spin on its own for a little span of time. Richard knew everything she knew. She wasn't alone.

The responsibility wasn't hers alone.

The door banged again, and she smelled hamburgers and fries. April and Nick were home. Richard was already up, making a call to figure out where the girl had contacted them from.

* * * *

 Rachel Starr Thomson

They were on the road in less than an hour: Richard, Mary, and Reese. He had traced the call to a property in the country forty miles east of the village and north of Lincoln. He had traced the name too. That hadn't been hard: Rick Brodie had been the subject of a missing persons report since his truck was found wrecked by the side of the highway with no trace of its driver three days before.

The same highway where two policemen had just been brutally, bloodily murdered.

Reese stewed on the news as they drove. She sat in the backseat, staring out at the countryside, thinking of Chris and Tyler.

Thinking more, she had to admit, of Chris. But it was Tyler she reached out to. Tyler she tried to find some connection with. She wished he had been around longer, had been able to master some of the abilities unique to Oneness. Other than their sense that he was still alive and okay, none of the cell had felt anything much from him since he and Chris had disappeared.

She allowed herself a sigh. Despite Richard's call to prayer the other night, despite the connection with the children's homes, despite it all, part of her had still been hoping that the boys had just gone off on their own somewhere—an extended fishing or hiking trip. And had been insensitive enough not to tell anyone.

Part of her had still been hoping they would just arrive home, browner and more muscled and stubborn about admitting they shouldn't have gone off and worried everyone like that.

They had enough pieces now that she couldn't cling to that hope anymore. Pieces—but nothing that fit together. Not yet. She had been forming a picture of what might be happening in Brass, with the teenager at the children's home, but Miranda had thrown the whole thing.

Miranda and the killings.

After Richard traced the call, she had called the twins. They had seen the news and were already on the alert. Alex had been around the house all day, they said, sullen and dark but not acting. He'd made it pretty clear he despised them both and wanted nothing to do with them, although they were trying to reach out in friendship or at least make him curious enough about them that he might try to recruit them or something. They didn't think he could see that they were Oneness.

It was right that they were in Brass, watching that front, but Reese wished they were here too. Watching her back. Brandishing their swords in the battle.

That battle was coming, she had no doubt in the least.

Their route took them by the site of the murders, and they slowed to a crawl. That whole side of the highway was blocked off; traffic was being routed over the median and down the other side. The highway wasn't usually inordinately busy, but enough truck traffic went through, and the highway had been closed so long, that it was backed up for over an hour.

Reese sat alert in the backseat, scanning the highway, the air, the police who were still there checking out the scene. The sense of evil was overpowering, and she could see blood on the pavement.

Splattered so far.

She shuddered and said a prayer.

And as the traffic finally began to pick up pace and Richard hit the gas again, he said, "Tyler was there."

"Are you sure?" Mary asked.

"Yes. I could feel his presence."

"He's not still there?"

"No, I don't think so."

"He's not . . ."

"He's not dead, no. Not one of the victims. But he was there."

Mary let the silence hang for a moment. "You think he saw it?"

"I hope not. I hope he closed his eyes."

Reese felt her eyes filling with tears. They stung.

Their exit wasn't much past the site of the killings. They drove onto a narrow two-lane highway into barren fields dotted with farms. It should be another good half-hour.

No wonder Miranda doesn't know where she lives, Reese thought as she looked around at the desolate stretch of country. She lives nowhere. It wasn't good farmland out here; it was too rocky. Farmers had to wrestle their crops up from the soil and coax them into maturity, walk them into harvest like fragile and needy children. But they did it, here as everywhere. Those who love the land will always find a way to work it.

Her mind went back to Tyler and Chris. How long had they been out here? What had they been doing? What on earth had even brought them out here?

And where were they now?

Oneness was Reese's joy, her identity and her whole life. But never had she been so frustrated by its limits. Frustrated that she couldn't just reach out and find Tyler in the Spirit, irrespective of distance. Frustrated that she couldn't draw Chris in, against his will, just make him part of her. She wanted that. Wanted him to be part of her. More than she was even willing to admit.

They found the farm without difficulty. It was down another road, one that essentially functioned as a private drive, but there was nothing else around and it was easy enough to spot. Two miles down that dirt road and around a bend, and they saw that the police had gotten there first.

Six squad cars sat in the wide drive at the front of an old farmhouse that sprawled more than it should, like it had been added onto more than once. Split-rail and stone fences marked off fields where corn, soy beans, and perhaps some other crops were growing. A green tractor sat abandoned in the soy field right next to the house, and the yard was likewise caught in still life—gardening tools lay in the large garden, kittens mewed where it looked like children had dropped them, a windmill creaked slowly in a barely existent breeze. The sense of heaviness and grief was palpable.

Richard pulled off to the side of the road rather than parking in the driveway. No people were in sight; everyone had to be inside.

"To pry or not to pry," he said.

"I don't think we have any choice," Mary answered.

"I wish we'd beaten the police."

"So do I."

Reese shifted in the backseat. "Should we wait till they leave? Seems a little unwise to connect ourselves to the community right now."

Richard was frowning. Reese saw the expression and realized it wasn't in reaction to anything she had said.

"What?" she asked.

"There's Oneness here," he said. "Can you feel it?"

Reese stilled herself and tried to reach out for connection. She felt nothing. "No."

"I'm not imagining it," Richard said, but he sounded like he was trying to assure himself. "But something's . . . wrong."

"There's a man dead here," Reese reminded him. "And at least one very scared little girl calling us for help. I'd say a few things are wrong."

The frown didn't ease up. Then he said, in a tone that made Reese stop and still her soul again, and forget to breathe for a moment, "What if David isn't the only one?"

Silence.

Mary cleared her throat. "What do you mean?"

"What if David isn't the only member of the Oneness to turn against us? There is Oneness here. I can feel it . . . him. But something about it is very wrong."

"Reese, the girl you talked to," Mary said. "Did you get any sense that she was one of us?"

"No," Reese said. "She didn't say anything to indicate she was, and I didn't feel any connection. She just sounded scared out of her head."

Richard opened his car door. "Let's get in there."

"What about the police?"

"We're going to assume they're on our side. The girl called them too."

"What are we going to tell them about why we're here?" Reese pushed.

Richard met her eyes. "The truth."

"I don't want to get the kid in trouble."

"She's already in trouble. Come on."

Mary and Reese followed Richard without another protest. He headed for the front door of the house like he belonged here, like he'd been called in on an investigation and everyone would know it. In the short time she'd known him, Reese had been impressed again and again by his authority. Richard did everything like he had a right to do it and went everywhere like he had a right to be there. As, it seemed, he did.

Gravel crunched under their feet, and the sounds of birds and insects in their summer symphony created a peace that was incongruous, totally out of keeping with the atmosphere of pregnant, dangerous stillness.

The wooden porch echoed under their steps as they climbed it, and Richard paused and listened at the door. They could all hear voices within. He looked at Mary and Reese, shrugged, and pushed the door open without knocking.

They walked right into the middle of a meeting. Roughly thirty people were quickly identifiable as the community: men, women, and children were all dressed conservatively, looking like something from another age, and except for a couple of the men and one of the women, they looked stunned. Reese's heart lurched as she realized how many of these were children—comparatively, the community really only had a handful of adults. One of the girls, a young teenager, fixed her eyes on Reese with an expression somewhere between hope and terror. Miranda, Reese thought. She was sitting glued to the side of an older woman who was most likely her mother. The woman's face was sweet and open, and marred at the moment by fear and by grief. The community members were all seated, arranged around several tables in a large dining room.

The police, by contrast, were standing. There were nine; Reese guessed others were elsewhere on the property. Their guns rode prominently in their holsters, and one had been writing notes.

At the head of one table, with two policemen standing on either side of him like guards, was a tall, black-bearded man whose eyes were blazing.

He was Oneness. Reese knew that in a heartbeat. Richard had been right.

And he had been right about something else: something about the man was very, very wrong.

Another David.

Her heart thought it might break.

He glared at them with hatred in his eyes. He knew who—what—they were. And he hated them.

Why? Reese thought in his direction. What are you think-ing? Why would you leave us—why would you fight against your own family, your own body?

"Who are you?" one of the police asked.

"My name is Richard . . . Richard Clark," Richard said, holding out his hand.

Hive　　　　　193

The officer didn't shake it. "What are you doing here?" he asked. "We're in the middle of an investigation."

"I'm aware of that. And I'm happy to answer your question, but maybe not in front of all these people."

The officer looked askance at him for a moment, then jerked his head toward the front door. "Step outside," he said.

He followed them out, and Reese and Mary introduced themselves. It felt odd to use their last names—they being a convention most of the Oneness gave up except when speaking formally with outsiders, as in this case. The policeman introduced himself as Lieutenant Mitch Jackson.

"Now, why are you here? And what's your connection to these people?"

Richard looked at Reese and nodded, indicating she should talk.

"I got a phone call this morning from one of the children here," she said. "A girl named Miranda. She told me a friend of ours had given her our number and that someone had died here, and she was scared."

"Someone did die here," the officer confirmed. "Truck driver named Rick Brodie. He's been missing for three days."

"That's the thing—so has our friend," Reese said. "The one who gave Miranda our number."

The officer's skepticism transformed instantly into interest. "So your friend was here?"

"He must have been. And possibly another. They've both been missing for the last three days."

"I don't remember any other report being filed," Jackson said.

     Rachel Starr Thomson

"We didn't file one. We thought they might just be on a fishing trip or something and hadn't mentioned it. But this isn't exactly fishing country."

"But you think they have some connection to Rick Brodie."

"Well, he was here, and so were they—or at least one of them."

The officer took out a pad and pen. "Can you give me their names?"

"Chris Sawyer and Tyler MacKenzie. Chris is the one who gave her the number."

"What do you know about their disappearance?"

"Not much," Reese said. "We . . . realized they weren't at home several days ago and had a bad feeling about it. We haven't been able to reach either of them since then. Chris has a cell phone, but we haven't been able to get through."

"What did he drive?"

"Excuse me?"

"His car," the officer said. "What did he drive?"

"Ford pickup," Richard said.

"Blue?"

"Yes. Why?"

Jackson pocketed his notepad and nodded. "I'd like you to come around the back and see if you can identify something for me. And then I'd like to know more about that phone call. Everything you can remember."

✳ ✳ ✳ ✳ ✳

They stood in the barn minutes later, staring wordlessly at the wreck of Chris's truck.

The front end was smashed up, though both seats were intact and it looked like anyone who had been inside should have been able to get away safely. The front right tire was twisted.

"They carried it here," Richard said, raising the end of the statement into a question.

"Seems that way. I don't think you could drive it with the front wheel well busted up like that."

Reese's brain was whirring, pulling pieces together. "The truck accident on the highway the other day. That was Rick Brodie's?"

"That's right. And this is the missing piece as to what exactly happened to him. The truck was wrecked but he wasn't there to ask about it, and no one had a good explanation for what had happened. We talked to dispatch at his company and they told us he seemed perfectly awake and aware just half an hour before we estimate the accident happened."

Staring at Chris's truck was making Reese sick to her stomach. She told herself, over and over, that he had gotten out. That they both had gotten out. Tyler wasn't dead, they knew that through the Oneness, and Chris had been fine enough to give Miranda a phone number.

But where were they now? They sure hadn't driven away.

"Have you searched the truck?" Richard asked.

"Not personally. We just found it an hour ago. Some of my colleagues had a look-see. You expecting anything?"

"Yeah," Richard said. "Chris's cell phone. That would explain why we haven't been able to reach him."

"Listen," Jackson said, "if your friend was mixed up in anything, best you tell us about it up front. A man is dead. Your friend's truck being here doesn't look good. They pulled it out of a wreck on the highway, left the truck but took the driver, and never called to report anything. I think you're smart enough to figure out the implications."

Richard answered slowly. "Chris and Tyler weren't involved in anything . . . not like you're thinking. But they were looking for someone who is. If you want a murderer, they aren't your guys. But it's possible that if you find them, you'll find your killer."

"Oh, we already have our killer," Jackson said.

"You what?"

Jackson clammed up, looking guilty. "Of course, that's up to the coroner to confirm."

"Those people?" Mary blurted out. "Those sweet people inside?"

"Not everyone in there is sweet," Jackson said. "Look, I might as well tell you . . . said a little too much already. As far as we can tell, Brodie died from something they gave him. They had him all bandaged up and taken care of, and he's only been dead not more than a day. Died this morning, is my guess. That's what they said. Most of them are playing totally innocent, but somebody in there knows what they were drugging him with and knows they gave him too much."

He shrugged. "Or maybe they just killed him in ignorance, and it was manslaughter. Any way you look at it, they shouldn't have been playing god."

Hive

Reese let her eyes wander back to the truck, at once so familiar and so terribly wrecked. In the dust and dirt of the barn it looked like it might have been there for ten years, but it was too new—too fresh. She started to picture the crash but wouldn't let herself go there.

She needed to talk to Miranda.

She turned to Lieutenant Jackson. "Sir, that girl, Miranda, called me. I'd like to talk to her."

"She might be a suspect," he warned. "Would you be willing to pass on what she tells you? If you get yourself mixed up in this, you'll end up talking to us one way or the other."

"I'm not against you," Reese said. "But sir, she's just a child."

He shook his head, weary. "But a child in the middle of a community that just killed someone. Suspect, accomplice, whatever. I'm just warning you that whatever you hear might not be able to stop with you."

Not that they could actually force anything out of her—out of any of them. Reese almost smiled to herself. They didn't know what they were dealing with, after all. Oneness generally did all they could not to involve local, human authorities in what they did. There were just too many factors they couldn't see. But Oneness also respected police, at least good ones. They were also, in a sense, servants.

"I'll help you bring justice any way I can," Reese said. "I just want to talk to her."

"Well, I don't think she's coming into custody, so there's no reason you can't once my fellow officers finish asking questions. At least not yet. Once we've had time to process some of the

     Rachel Starr Thomson

formalities, there's a good chance these folks will all end up in custody for a while. Personally, I'm more inclined to see most of them as victims. But we don't know yet."

"You're local police," Richard said. "Have you dealt with these people before? Do you know anything abut them?"

"We've been out here once or twice. Occasional complaints from neighbours, but nothing substantiated. Seems most folks just don't like how isolated these people are. They get an attitude about it. One neighbour called us and reported child abuse, but there was nothing like that going on that we could find. I've always been inclined to sympathize with most of them." He sniffed. "Personally, I don't like their leader—Jacob. But he's never been in trouble before."

He looked back at the truck. "At least, nothing like this."

"Now, before you go." He pulled out his pad again. "If you don't mind, I'll take your names and numbers. We may want to be in touch again. In case anything comes up about your friends."

Richard nodded and took the pad and pen. Reese tuned them out, letting her gaze rest on the truck again and her heart cry out for Chris and Tyler as her spirit tried to reach, tried to find them, clawed with frustration at the distance and the gap and what Chris wasn't . . .

She signed her own name and wrote down the cell house number almost mindlessly.

Jackson led them back out of the barn, and they blinked in the strong summer sunlight. A couple of policemen they hadn't seen before were standing around the squad cars; one was radio-ing something. "Find anything?" Jackson called.

"Nothing," one of them said. "Just that truck."

Just the truck.

As she headed toward the house again, hoping for the conversation inside to end soon so she could speak with Miranda, Reese let her heart reach out one more time.

* * * * *

Tyler refused to open his eyes

He could not, would not, put any picture to the things he had heard after the police came.

His whole body was shaking. He could still smell it. Still feel it. But not see it. He had closed his eyes; he had refused to look.

The children's jingle kept running through his head: Hear no evil, see no evil, speak no evil.

See no evil, see no evil, he told himself.

Don't look into the demon's eyes.

Don't look.

Don't see the blood.

Don't look at his face.

Don't think about it.

It was impossible not to think about it.

"Tyler," Chris's voice grated.

He ignored it. Just kept singing to himself. See no evil, see no evil, hear no evil . . .

 Rachel Starr Thomson

"Tyler!"

He shook his head, shaggy hair plastered against his face from the sweat, surprised that he could move that much. His limbs still felt so heavy. He didn't know where he was. Were they still in the truck? Still going somewhere? To the hive?

To more demons?

He didn't know why he had thought everything would be okay. Why he had thought Oneness could win. Why he had thought love was stronger than hate. And killing. Death. Murder. The kind of cruelty that revelled in blood.

And through all his confusion and pain, he could hear Chris calling him, and something else.

Something deeper, and farther away.

Something that didn't speak to his ears but to his spirit.

And yet it had a voice, and he recognized it.

Reese.

Reese was calling to him.

He opened his eyes.

Chris was sitting across from him. They were both seated, propped up against—truck walls? The inside of a trailer? Yes, he thought. They hadn't been moved.

The truck itself was not moving.

He stared at Chris, momentarily unable to understand why he could hear Reese when she was not there in front of him.

"Tyler, you have to wake up," Chris said in a low, urgent voice. There was something wrong with his face—something patterned, speckled.

It was blood. Not his. Someone else's. There had been blood everywhere . . .

He closed his eyes again.

"Tyler, dang it, listen to me. I can't fight this . . . whatever it is. This thing. This demon."

Was Chris's voice shaking? Yes, it was. He sounded scared. Tyler had never heard him sound scared before.

"Tyler, I can't fight it, but you can. You have the weapon for it. That sword thing you carry. The ability to sense and see things. You're Oneness. You have got to wake up and act like it."

"I'm not enough," Tyler croaked. "I'm too young. Too . . . I'm not enough."

"You don't have to be. You're not alone. Remember? Never alone. That's what you said. You people. All of you."

Tyler opened his eyes again, and Chris locked his gaze. "You can do this, and you have to do it. Not just for us. For Reese. And Mum. And Richard and Mary and April. You're one of them, and if you don't do something, they're all going to get attacked by this thing. Remember? We left the village to track down the hive. Well, we found it. So you can't quit on me now."

His words were brave, big. Far more full of courage than his eyes. But he had recited all their names like a litany, like a charge. Because for Chris, nothing mattered so much as those he wanted to protect. And he hoped it would stir up the same determination in Tyler.

So they could . . . something. Fight?

Martyr themselves?

But there was Reese . . .

He concentrated on the sense, deep inside, that she was calling him. He closed his eyes and tried to focus in on it, to hear it, to embrace the voice. And he found that he could. It wasn't an illusion. Reese, closer than a sister or a mother, as much a part of him as breathing, was calling him and had somehow found him here, in the darkness, in his fear. He wasn't alone.

He really wasn't.

So he didn't have to be enough.

"Reese is calling me," he said again.

"What? Right now?"

"Yes."

"You can hear her?"

"And . . . feel her."

There was pain in Chris's eyes. Pain Tyler didn't have to guess at.

Love hurt sometimes, even when you weren't quite ready to admit it existed, or how deeply it mattered to you.

Outside, they both heard footsteps and voices.

In a moment they wouldn't be alone anymore.

"Tyler, you have to fight," Chris said.

And Tyler nodded. And said, "I know."

* * * * *

Reese found Miranda minutes after the police had pulled away, with Jacob and his wife and a few others in custody, and pulled her aside. "I'm Reese," she said. "You called me. I'm here."

"You came so fast," Miranda said. Her eyes were watery, and she was pale and trembling. Reese couldn't imagine what she was going through.

"I came as soon as I could. I would have found you earlier, but I had to wait until the police left."

Miranda nodded. She was probably fourteen or fifteen, but at the moment she looked like a little girl. Lost, terrified. Growing up by the second and not at all ready for it.

"They asked so many questions," Miranda whispered.

"Did you answer them?"

"I let the grownups talk."

"Did they ask you?"

"Some things."

"And you told them what they asked?"

"Some things."

Reese sighed and looked around, spotting a swing under a wide oak tree in the yard. "Will you sit with me? In the shade over there? Would that be okay?"

Miranda nodded. She was clasping and unclasping her hands, and Reese wished she had a doll or something she could give her—something she could clutch and keep her nerves steady.

As they walked, just as they were about to seat themselves, Reese said, "So how did you meet Chris?"

"They were here," Miranda whispered. The whispers seemed so unnecessary in the sun. They should be sipping lemonade and talking about nothing. Enjoying a beautiful summer day.

Not potentially ripping each other's worlds apart.

Silently, Reese vowed that no matter how much destruction came on this girl's world in connection with her, she would help her put it back together again. As much as was possible.

"Did you tell the police that?"

"No, they didn't ask."

"Okay." She paused. "When were they here?"

"They left today, late in the morning. We weren't supposed to know. They had to meet with Jacob, and he packed them in a truck and sent them away with . . ."

Her voice dropped even lower, so low and so indistinct Reese almost couldn't hear her. "Him."

"Why were they here?" Reese asked, holding her own voice as steady as she could.

"They were in an accident," Miranda said. "They both got banged up pretty bad. Chris broke his arm. Like Rick . . . Rick broke his leg. We brought them all here, away from the highway, because Lorrie found them when she was out driving and she called Jacob and said they were hurt. We brought them here to take care of them."

Her eyes filled with tears. "We were just giving them medicine to take away their pain. He wasn't supposed to die. I don't . . . I don't think . . ."

"It's okay," Reese said, laying a hand on the girl's hand. "I know you didn't want to kill anyone."

"I didn't give it to him that time," Miranda said. "Usually I did. I was helping Lorrie with the medicines and the food and things. Learning to take care of sick people. I want to be a nurse. Or a midwife. To help people."

Her eyes grew wider, and her hands shook. "Now I don't know what's going to happen."

"Shh," Reese said, taking the girl in her arms. "It's going to be okay. I know it doesn't seem like it now, but this . . . this will pass. And you'll learn to do all you wanted to do. I know you will."

"They said we poisoned him," Miranda said, dissolving into sobs. Her shoulders shook, but she hardly made a sound. "They made it sound like we did it on purpose."

"They're just trying to learn what really happened," Reese said.

"But if they find out! I don't want them to take her away."

"Who?"

"My mother. She . . . she gave him the medicine. Last night. And he didn't wake up this morning. We didn't know until after Tyler and Chris went . . ."

"Shh," Reese said. She didn't want the child to stop talking—but to stop hurting, yes, to stop shaking and feeling the terror of having her universe ripped apart and threatened from within. "It's going to be okay," she said again.

She had heard somewhere, a long time ago, that if you encountered someone in a traumatic situation—in a natural disaster or a terrorist attack, for example—that you shouldn't say "It's going to be okay." Because you just couldn't promise that.

She knew she couldn't promise it this time either. For all she knew, Miranda's mother was a murderer, and nothing would ever be okay again.

But she didn't say that. She just kept saying what she hoped, wanted, to be true. And projected it out as far as she could so that it touched her world too, and Tyler and Chris, and the hive, and whatever was wrong with the Oneness that it could produce men like David and Jacob and invite demons into its midst.

She wouldn't allow herself to think about the horrible murders on the highway, the ones no one had said a word about since they got here. They weren't sure the police who had been called to look into the community even knew about them, and they weren't going to say. No sense in complicating the situation on the ground anymore than it already was.

But she knew it wasn't unconnected.

Reese held the girl close and let her cry on her shoulder for a few minutes. Then slowly, carefully, she asked, "Why did Chris give you my number?"

"Because I was scared," Miranda said. And now there was a new tone in her voice. Guilt.

"Do you want to explain that?"

"I was supposed to be watching them all at night," Miranda said. "Making sure they didn't need anything. I was supposed to call Jacob if they woke up or needed something because we aren't supposed to be with men alone. Especially not at night. But Tyler woke up and came out, and I had gone . . . gone downstairs, when I wasn't supposed to, and when I came back up he was up, and I knew . . . I thought Jacob wouldn't like it. So I didn't tell him. But I was scared. And I tried to go to sleep in the hallway but then I was having dreams, and they were all bad, and Chris got up and came out too, and I knew I was going to be in so much trouble if Jacob found out I was just talking to them and not telling anyone. But Chris is so nice, and he knew I was scared, and he said if I ever needed anything or got in trouble, I should call you. And he gave me your number."

While she was still wondering about that, a look of even stronger guilt came over Miranda's face.

"What?" Reese asked.

"I drugged him extra hard," Miranda said. 'So he would sleep long in the morning and maybe forget to tell anyone about talking to me."

Alarm came over Reese. "You did what? Don't you know that could have been dangerous?"

"I knew what I was doing," Miranda said, defensive, but then the reality of their situation came back over her and she dissolved into tears again. "I don't know how it could have happened! Mama is smart, and she knows better than to . . ."

She trailed off.

"Miranda," Reese said, pushing back a little and looking the girl in the face, "I need you to tell me everything you know. Everything. When you called me, you said they killed someone. And you called the police. Why?"

"Because he was dead."

Reese recalled the girl's tone on the phone and decided to push. "And you don't really believe it was an accident."

Her features hardened, and her mouth made a straight line.

Reese sighed. "Okay. I won't push. But tell me what hap-pened to Tyler and Chris. You want to help them, don't you?"

She was still more hesitant, more close-lipped than before but the appeal obviously had some effect. "I told you . . . they got in trouble with Jacob, and he sent them away."

"You said with 'him.' Who were you talking about?"

And Miranda did something totally unexpected.

She shuddered.

Reese sat up a little straighter. "Miranda," she said firmly, "you need to tell me everything you know."

"He comes to talk to Jacob," Miranda said. "I used to think he was handsome. But now he just scares me so much."

"Who?"

"Clint. His name is Clint."

"Does he have a last name?"

"I don't know."

The girl from the phone call who didn't know her own address was back. Reese tried to keep down her frustration and be patient, but it took every ounce of effort. "What do you know about him?"

"He . . . he scares me. I wanted to marry him. Jacob said he was a fine young man. He comes to meet with him and they talk forever and ever and ever. Some of the other men have been meeting with him too. They talk about spiritual things, Jacob says. But sometimes they come away and they're all . . . something's not right with them. Their eyes."

"Miranda, tell me what you know."

"I saw once." Her eyes were big as saucers. "I wasn't supposed to. The meeting was just for the men. We girls are supposed to stay out. Even the ladies are supposed to stay out. But I wanted to know . . . and I thought Clint was so handsome, and they were talking about marrying me to him, so I went and snuck into the loft once when they were meeting in the barn and watched and listened." She shuddered again, and her eyes filled with tears. "It was so horrible."

Reese rubbed the girl's back between her shoulders and waited. She could be patient. She silently sent up prayer, connecting, drawing strength from the Spirit and willing it to transfer to this child somehow. "They said they were just going to pray, but it wasn't like Jacob used to teach us all how to pray. They sat in a circle with candles and there was blood."

"What do you mean there was blood?"

"Clint brought it with him. In a bottle. And he put it on all the men's foreheads. It stunk, and it scared me. And then he started chanting and it got so dark. It was already nighttime, and the lamps were lit . . . I don't know how it got dark like that. And then it was like something else was there."

Reese asked carefully, "Did anyone seem different after that?"

"Yeah. All the men. Their eyes went all strange, and they've been . . . they scare me. I don't like to be around them anymore."

"All the men?" Reese asked. "Were they all in on it?"

"No, just some," Miranda amended. "Just three, and Jacob."

Reese bit her lip. "What about Jacob? Did he change too?"

"He's the same. But I'm more scared of him than I used to be. He was so angry with Tyler and Chris the other day. He gets angry with all of us. He says we're supposed to be different from the world, but we're just like them, wanting to be like everybody out there instead of following God's ways. But we don't. I don't think. I think we all want to do what's right."

"Miranda, what happened in that barn wasn't God's way."

"I didn't think so."

"Are you the only one who knows about all this?"

"No, my mother knows. I told her. I shouldn't have, probably, but I was so scared that night."

"What did she say?"

"She didn't say very much. She just said things would be all right. But I don't think she likes it either. She's been not very happy. And Lorrie is mad at her all the time."

Reese nodded. "It's good that you told her. You should keep talking to her, whatever happens. You don't have to be alone."

"But Jacob doesn't like us to talk about some things."

"Like what things?"

Miranda paused. "Him. Or things we aren't happy with. He says we complain and judge and that we need to respect his authority."

Reese bit her tongue. "Just keep talking to your mom. That's why you have a mom. So she can help you make sense of things."

Miranda nodded but didn't look convinced. Reese marveled at how much confusion and guilt one man could introduce into a young life. But that was typical. Jacob wanted control, and confusion and guilt were two of the main tools of control. She said a silent prayer that this child would be set free—her and her mother and all the others in this community, even those who were already demonized, who were already being drawn into the hive.

"Okay, now listen," Reese said. "I'm going to ask you more questions, and I need you tell me everything you know. But you should know that I'm going to tell the police what you tell me. This is not wrong, Miranda. It's the right thing to do. You need to be honest so that Chris and Tyler don't get hurt. Tell me everything you remember about them being taken away."

Miranda stared at her, and she started to shake. Reese locked into her eyes. "Someone is already dead," she reminded the girl. "You can help me stop Chris and Tyler from dying too. This isn't a game. And you know this time what's right and what's wrong. You know it isn't right that Rick Brodie died, and you know it isn't right that my friends were taken away. Listen to what you know. And tell me."

"Clint was here," Miranda said. "I saw him come into the house. Jacob was talking to Chris and Tyler in the dining room, and they were all yelling and mad at each other. Clint was listening outside the door. Then he went inside and everything got quiet, and then I could just hear him and Jacob talking. He said he would take them away and Jacob wouldn't have to worry about them anymore. He said he would make everything disappear. I got scared because I shouldn't be listening, so I ran around the house, and I saw a truck out front and some other men. I don't know who they were."

"How many other men?"

"Just two."

"What kind of truck?"

     Rachel Starr Thomson

"Like a moving van . . . not a very big one. I didn't want the men to see me so I hid in the bushes. And then I saw Clint and Jacob and Nathan carrying Chris and Tyler out, and they put them in the back of the truck. And then Clint climbed in after them, and they shut the door and then the other men got into the front of the truck and drove it away."

She was shaking harder than ever.

"And then what happened?" Reese asked gently.

"And then Mama came out wailing and crying because Rick Brodie died."

"And then you called the police?"

Miranda nodded, tears streaking down her face suddenly. "I didn't know what else to do. I'm not supposed to use the phone. I'm not even supposed to know where it is. But I do because . . . well, because. So I went and called 911 and told them about the death. And then I called you."

"You did the right thing," Reese said.

"I don't know," Miranda said. "I think maybe I ruined everything. They took Jacob and Lorrie away, and they're going to come back. No one is allowed to go anywhere right now."

"I know you feel like you betrayed them," Reese said, "but all you did was tell the truth. The truth is going to help. In the end, even if it hurts for a while, it will help. Can you believe that?"

She was trembling so hard that her teeth chattered. "I don't know."

"Well," Reese said, "I do. I understand what it's like to be part of a family, of a community like this. I know how it feels to do things they don't like. But the truth is going to help all of you.

Even Jacob and Lorrie. And especially you and your mother."

"What if we all go to jail?"

"Then it will probably feel like your world has ended. But it won't have. Not really."

Miranda looked away, and as she did she gradually calmed down. Finally she looked back, surveying Reese's face in the green shade of the tree. "You're a lot like Tyler," she said.

"Yes, I am."

"You're both like Jacob."

Reese thought about that for a minute. "In some ways, yes."

"But you don't scare me, and he does."

"Jacob has made some choices that should scare you," Reese said. "I know it's hard for you to think about him like that, but you know he's been doing things that are wrong. He's been bringing in people and powers that aren't safe. Pay attention to that fear. Pay attention to what you're feeling. It's not wrong."

She stood. "I have to go," she said. "I have to find my friends. Thank you for your help. You can call us again—you, or your mother, or anybody who needs us. And I'll come back and check on you. I promise."

"Even if I go to jail?"

Reese smiled. "Even then."

　　　　Rachel Starr Thomson

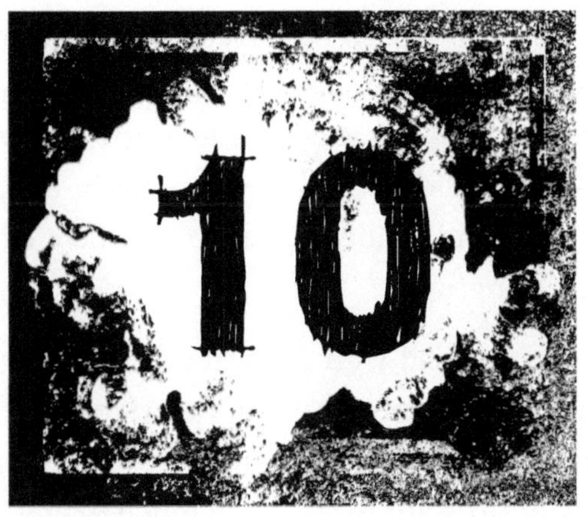

Tony's head was buried in a math textbook, staring cross-eyed at algebraic equations he could make absolutely no sense of, when he felt Angelica's eyes boring into his back and turned around.

From a desk behind him in study hall, she gestured toward an empty seat.

Alex was gone.

He had been there two seconds ago . . . Tony had turned around to check, pretending to be looking at a clock on the back wall. But now he realized that he could feel the teen's absence; the low-lying, under-the-surface tension that filled the air when he was there had lifted. It was so undercover that the change was barely perceptible. But it was there.

Both twins raised their hands at the same time. The teacher raised an eyebrow. "Yes?"

"Bathroom?" they blurted in unison.

"Go ahead."

They spilled into the hall at the same time and looked both ways. Alex was nowhere to be seen. Sharing the same instinct, they turned on their heels and headed for the double doors at the end of the hall—the ones that let out into the schoolyard in the back. They didn't think he was still in the school. And they didn't think he would be out front where anyone would notice him exiting.

A day on duty had won them no friendship with the boy from the home. He ignored them, occasionally casting scowls in their direction, and they hung out trying to interest him but failing. They didn't want to show too much interest lest they tip him off to their true identity. As it was, it was playing with fire to be Oneness in the presence of demons. Both could lie low if they wanted to—keeping to the shadows, essentially—but you never knew when a wrong movement was going to give you away. Dr. Smith treated them like anyone else in the home, and Susan and Valerie did likewise. This, their second day at school, had been hardly more revealing. Alex kept to himself, showed little to no interest in any of his classmates and zero aptitude for anything scholastic. He spent most of his time with music in his ears and his eyes focused on something in his own head that no one else really wanted to know about.

Tony and Angelica had both kept a close eye on anyone Alex interacted with, hoping to find more of the hive. They did notice that one of the teenage girls seemed to make a special point of avoiding him, and Angelica would have put that down to normal adolescent dislike if it wasn't for the faint presence of fear in the girl's eyes. But she showed no sign of being demonized herself.

Disappointing, considering they had hoped to find more of

     Rachel Starr Thomson

the hive in the school. Of course it was possible that there were more, that the hive was in fact spreading through this ready-made social network, but that its members weren't the type to be in summer school. Alex himself wasn't that type; Dr. Smith forced him to be here, as was obvious from everything in his demeanour. Judging from how poorly he seemed to perform in every class, it was obvious the doctor was wise to send him. He could probably use all the help he could get.

But now he was gone, and finally, both twins knew deep in their gut, the chase was on.

They made it to the yard in time to catch a fleeting glimpse of black disappearing into the woods across the fence on the far side, past a basketball court and stretch of ground where the track-and-fielders met. The woods weren't much, just a long patch of greenery in the middle of the town that hadn't been bought and developed, but it was enough to hide in or escape through. The twins exchanged a glance and then wordlessly broke into a trained, silent run, straight across the schoolyard. They risked Alex turning around and seeing them, but he shouldn't expect that anyone was following, and it was a better risk to take than losing him completely because they were slowed down trying to stay out of sight.

One after the other they jumped the fence and stood in a crouch, not saying a word, looking and listening for any sign of the direction he had taken. The woods weren't their usual terri-tory—they had done most of their demon hunting in the city haunts of Lincoln. But the dark air and the eerie silence in the trees felt familiar. Whatever was in Alex was manifesting itself more strongly now, not trying to hide. It left an aura behind it: that unmistakable mix of fascination, beckoning, and horror.

Tony led the way, picking a direction straight through the trees. There was a barely discernible path that might have been nothing more than a deer track or the vague waymaking of root and tree trunks, or might have been used by human beings before. Angelica followed hard on his heels. As soon as their ears picked up the sound of someone ahead of them, they slowed their steps and hung back. The trick now was to follow without being heard.

They didn't want to catch Alex. Not until he led them wherever he was trying to go. Not until he led them to others.

They had done this before. Tracked this very hive before. Followed demons and demonic activity, trying to get to the centre of it. Once, it had led Reese to the warehouse, with Tony breathlessly at her side, and Patrick, their friend who had died in the fight, watching their backs. The warehouse had reeked of death and evil and rot, horror crowding out fascination; it had housed the core—an enormous gathering of demons drawing strength from something and using that strength to go out and perpetuate the hive. The evil of David's betrayal, though none of them knew it then.

They had hoped, when they went into that warehouse swinging their swords and fighting like crazed warriors from some bygone age, that they were destroying the hive once and for all. They had been wrong. David pulled them back and stopped the forward advance of their attack, long enough, apparently, to allow the core to regroup after the battle where Patrick died.

One thing was for sure, with so many demons gathering in one place—thousands, Tony thought—the potential of the hive had to be staggering. They would not come, not in such force, if they did not believe they could find and possess people enough

 Rachel Starr Thomson

for all of them. People like Alex, bent on destroying themselves. People like the man who had impersonated Dr. Smith, bent on destroying others—children like Nick and good men like Vince Smith himself. And ideally, they would find people with connections: people who were part of homes, schools, communities, so that the evil could spread. Demonized people often isolated themselves, or were isolated by their communities, but that worked against the demonic drive and frustrated them. They wanted everyone.

They wanted, badly, to annihilate themselves, and take everyone—the whole human race, and the whole universe held together by the human race—down with them.

The woods grew darker toward the centre, where the trees were oldest and tallest and most tangled together, and the aura of demonic personality left a stronger stink in the darkness. And then they thinned out, and the twins paused before stepping onto a cracked sidewalk on a residential street. Alex hadn't seen them. He was halfway up the block, heading who knew where at a faster clip than before.

Then, abruptly, he stopped at an intersection and waited, fidgeting, next to a stop sign. Half a block down, Tony and Angelica tried to duck out of sight, hiding behind a parked car. Alex was looking every way, clearly not wanting anyone to see him, clearly concerned that someone would.

He went rigid and stood up straighter. Tony tensed—he'd seen them.

Or not. Seconds later, a car pulled up to the stop sign, and Alex jumped in. The car, looking like something out of the '60s but in sleek, prime condition, roared away.

The twins stood up, abandoning their hiding place in shock. They weren't convinced Alex hadn't spotted them. But what had just happened? How had they lost him so quickly?

"Did you get a license number?" Tony asked.

"No. Just didn't see that coming fast enough."

"Guess I can't blame you for that. I didn't either."

The car was long gone—by the time they reached the stop sign and turned up the next street, there was no sign of it. And no anything to indicate where it might have gone.

Tony kicked a fire hydrant.

"Like that's gonna help," Angelica commented.

"You got any better ideas?"

"Yeah, go back to the home and see if Dr. Smith knows anything he hasn't told us about where Alex goes and who he sees. And then leave at least one of us there."

"Why? I want to keep hunting."

"The home is under attack. Maybe if one of us stays there, the prey will come to us. Anyway, Alex's being gone isn't a good thing. He's with them, almost guaranteed, and who knows what that means to everyone else."

"Fine," Tony acknowledged. "You're right. Think we're going to get in trouble for not being in school?"

"With the school, yes. With the home—only if nothing happens that requires our help."

Just following their feet and their vague memory of the direction they had taken on the bus the past two days, they opted

     Rachel Starr Thomson

not to go back through the woods to the school but just to keep wandering through the residential neighbourhoods until they found the children's home. Both moody and frustrated, they didn't say anything.

Until Tony held out his arm and stopped Angelica midstep.

"Do you feel that?" he asked.

As one, they turned their heads to face a house on their left. A moving truck sat in the driveway, and a nondescript wooden fence, higher than eye-level, surrounded the yard. The house itself had that old, slightly overgrown look—like whoever lived there couldn't really be bothered to trim grass or oil hinges. But it wasn't the house that really drew their attention. It was something beyond, behind it—like the house was just a film, a haze with a very different reality diffused behind it.

For some reason, both twins suddenly felt as though the ground might drop out from beneath their feet.

Angelica spotted it first—through a crack in the fence. The shine of car wax—the car that had picked up Alex. It was here.

The Oneness believed that their steps were caught up in a bigger picture than one person could see, something sewn up and patched together by the Spirit itself. They called it a plan. Sometimes plans were nothing but darkness and confusion to understand. Other times, they were so obvious you could be staring them in the face.

Being here, now, finding the car, this was not a coincidence.

Tony's face went ashen.

"What?"

"David's here. I can feel him."

She knew it was true the moment he said it—and she realized she'd felt his presence all along. It was just so familiar, so much a part of them, that despite everything that had happened it didn't call attention to itself right away. But now that she was aware of it, it froze her in her tracks.

"Can he feel us too?" she asked, her voice faint.

"Get out of here, now," Tony said. "They're coming."

They turned and ran, and the ground dropped out or the sky fell, they weren't really sure which—but their footsteps were swallowed up in tangible darkness, blinding them, and they yelled and swung the swords that were present in their hands as demons flocked down and beat around their heads and shoulders. The ground reached up like hands and sucked at their feet, pulling them down to their knees, grasping at their arms, the air growing heavy and weighting them down, pressing on their shoulders, like the whole atmosphere was trying to swallow them up. Angelica tried to swing her sword but couldn't; it was all she could do to keep her feet.

Dimly they knew this was not the work of demons alone; demonic power did not extend to the earth. That took man and man's authority. This was what humanity had long called witchcraft and feared, even as some practiced it and became worse than demons.

This time they had found more than a core.

     Rachel Starr Thomson

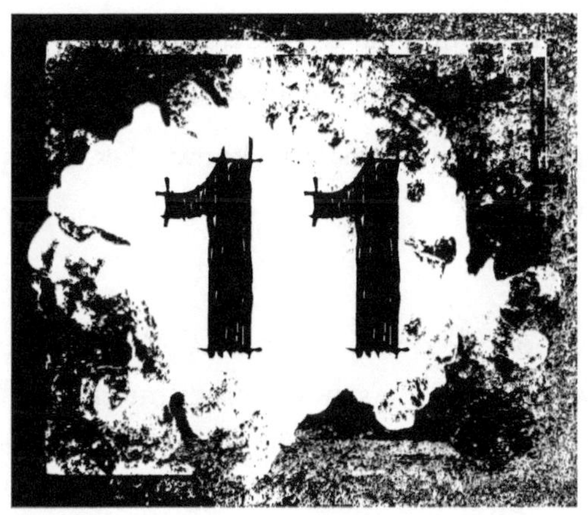

When April and Nick came back from an excursion down to the harbour to watch the boats coming in and out, the phone was ringing. She rushed to it while Nick took his time getting his shoes off at the front door.

"Hello?"

"Hello, is this Reese?" It was a man's voice, unfamiliar.

"No, I'm sorry, she's out."

"I've been calling for the last hour trying to reach her. Do you know how I can get hold of her?"

"Who is this?"

April's heart was stopping of its own accord. She knew who it was. Who had it had to be. Dr. Vincent Smith—the real Dr. Vincent Smith.

He confirmed her suspicion.

"She left this morning to follow up an emergency call," April said. "But maybe I can help you."

"Maybe you'll have to. Do you know anything about the twins?"

"You mean about what they're doing? Yes . . . Reese told me she posted them at your home to keep an eye on things."

He sounded relieved that she knew. "Yes, that's right. They disappeared today."

"They what?"

"The school called two hours ago. Alex, the boy they were trying to watch, left the school sometime during first period. They must have followed—they excused themselves for a break and never came back."

"Does anyone know where they went?"

"No one saw them leave, and they haven't called. I've been trying to reach Reese ever since the school alerted me. I know they may just be tracking Alex, but I thought you should know something is up."

"Thank you," April said. "You were right to call."

"Did you see the news? About the murders on the highway?"

"Yes."

He was silent. She closed her eyes. "Yes, we think they're connected to whatever's going on with Alex."

"Do you have a good reason to think that?"

"Just faith that nothing is coincidence. We're dealing with demons, and this much demonic activity in one region is almost certainly connected."

"You don't think what happened on the highway was just the result of someone deranged."

     Rachel Starr Thomson

She almost smiled. "What do you think causes that kind of derangement?"

"Point taken."

"You wouldn't be asking if you didn't think they were connected."

He hesitated. Then, "I found something in Alex's room. I'm disturbed. Drawings."

Art. April knew all about that. "Drawings of murder?"

"Butchery might be a better word."

"Doctor, if you hear from the twins or get any idea of where they are, will you call us please?"

"Of course. I'd like your help in dealing with all this."

April hung up and stood at the counter in deep thought. It took her a few minutes to notice Nick standing patiently, staring at her.

"Sorry," she said. "Do you need something?"

"I want to draw. Will you help me? I need you to show me how."

For a fleeting moment, April wondered what charcoal and paper could unleash from this boy's soul.

She shuddered.

"Yes, I can help you. Bring your art stuff here."

She hardly saw him go. She watched the phone a moment, willing it to ring, and then picked it up herself and called Diane. The call was short, just a quick request and a few cryptic remarks. And then she hung up and sat at the table with her head in her hands.

They were too split up. Everyone somewhere the others weren't. The twins who knew where. Reese and Richard and Mary off in the country somewhere, trying to track down Chris and Tyler, who were . . . much, much too far away. Too hidden. Calling all ships, April thought. Everyone please come home.

Nick had been attempting a wolf but didn't know how to shade it properly. April showed him a few things, distracted, and almost leaped up to answer the door when Diane arrived.

Diane looked pointedly at Nick.

"Nick, please go up . . ." April trailed off. "Never mind. You can stay."

"Do you really think that's wise?"

"He lives here. He's going to pick up on things. He might as well be in this."

"All right." Diane looked dubious, but she sat down across the table from Nick and didn't insist that he go anywhere.

"The twins followed that boy, Alex, somewhere. They all left the school hours ago. Dr. Smith is worried and he called wanting to talk to Reese. He says he found drawings in his room—Alex's room. And they were disturbing enough that he thinks Alex is connected with the highway murders."

Diane groaned lightly. "No terrible surprise there."

"I want to do something. I hate it that everyone else is out except us."

Nick's head was down. He had flipped a page in his sketchbook and started something new, working with his nose almost on the paper like he knew he wasn't supposed to be here and was making a point of concentrating on his artwork so they would know he wasn't really listening all that closely.

"Where would we even go?" Diane asked. "We don't know where anyone is. Better to stay here and wait for someone to call."

"We could go to the children's home."

"And do what? Wait for the twins to come back? When they get there, they'll be back . . . no real need for us to go too."

"Maybe they won't come back."

"You're afraid."

"You saw the news. You saw everything they would show and say and you heard how much they wouldn't show or say. And that phone call this morning . . . people are dying. This isn't a small attack. If the twins followed Alex, and Alex had something to do with those murders . . ."

"I hear what you're saying. I just don't know what we can do."

April saw the anguish in Diane's eyes and stopped talking. For a moment she had forgotten that this woman's son was right in the centre of everything—was still missing, was somehow connected to at least one death, was completely unreachable and was not even One.

"I'm sorry. I'm being insensitive."

"No, you're right. We should try to do something."

"I don't really know how to fight battles. I've lived here most of my life as Oneness. War is Reese's thing. Reese and the twins."

"Then it's good that they're the ones out there." Diane covered her face and said nothing.

Outside, tires crunched gravel.

Diane dropped her hands and looked at April, startled. They both jumped up at once. Reese was home. Or Chris was home. Or . . .

Diane got to the door first and froze with her hand on the knob, looking out the window.

"Who is it?" April asked. She rushed to Diane's side, pushed aside the lace curtain covering the small window on the door, and stopped breathing.

It was Dr. Vincent Smith.

The first one.

"Nick, get upstairs and lock yourself in your room. Now."

He looked up from his intent work, his jaw slack.

"Now!"

Gathering his stuff quickly, Nick pushed it all under his arm and ran from the room. April regretted chasing him off like that. But she could feel a sword forming in her hand. She stepped back from the door. Diane positioned herself just behind her.

Before she stepped away from the curtain, she'd seen the gun in the man's hand.

Heart pounding, she waited for him to come in.

There was no point in trying to stop him or slow him down.

He was here for a showdown, and she knew it.

Wanted it, almost.

She'd been complaining that they couldn't go out to meet the enemy. So it was fair that the enemy would come to her.

      Rachel Starr Thomson

The door knob turned, and he entered. Gun first. Ready to fire.

He smiled. "Put that sword away."

The weapon had formed itself fully in April's hand.

"You're not really trained to use it," whatever was in him said. "Before you could get close enough to cast me out, he would pull the trigger and you would die."

April's knuckles were turning white. She didn't put the sword away, but equally she didn't make a move to use it. He was right—she couldn't possibly win this fight.

It was so much simpler when demons came in the bodies of animals, or in their own ethereal, only half-physical forms.

"Let him go," April said. "Face me yourself."

"I am facing you myself," the creature answered. "You act as though I'm holding him prisoner. I'm not. His will and mine are one. He would shoot you even if I wasn't in him."

The man smiled—a stretched-out, nasty smile that looked as though something behind his skin was moving it. His eyes moved methodically to Diane. "I didn't expect to find you both here. Very well. Saves me a drive."

"What do you want with us?" Diane demanded. Her voice shook, but she spoke clearly. She had faced possessed men before, but not like this. The thugs who had worked with David had been blank, stupid. The teenagers who killed Douglas had been out of their minds. This man was malignant. Present. Very much evil, and very much joined to the spiritual power that inhabited him.

The demon was speaking for the moment, but Diane and

April both sensed that the man did not mind.

This was the real danger, the real horror of a hive—not that some men would become controlled by demons, but that some men would give themselves over so completely that there was little difference between the two, and the demon would strengthen the man where he lacked and the man strengthen the demon where it lacked. It was a mockery, a perversion of the Oneness in its unity with the Spirit. A mockery designed to unravel and destroy the very universe the Oneness held together, plunging it into chaos and eternal darkness.

Demons alone could never achieve their goal. They were too scattered, too divided, too dependent on physical forms, and too limited in their understanding.

With men, they were capable of uniting. Forming a vision and truly working toward it. Controlling the earth and mastering themselves.

"I want two things," the demon said. He pointed at April. "Your life."

And then at Diane. "And your company."

Diane looked at April, alarmed. "I don't know what you mean, but you're not going to get either."

"Oh, I am. I am going to get both. You cannot actually stop me, you see."

He took a step forward, and then jerked as though he had walked into something invisible. Arrested, he glared at them both.

"What is this?" he hissed.

They looked at one another, wordless—unable to answer the

    Rachel Starr Thomson

question because they didn't know the answer themselves. The man's whole body tensed and jerked as he tried to force himself forward, but it seemed he was blocked by something. "It can't be," the demon said, its voice rising. "He isn't here! We made sure he wasn't here!"

April nearly laughed.

Richard.

Prayer.

"It's prayer," she said. "He built a wall."

The demon scowled at her, and she knew she was right.

But the moment of relief at being protected passed as the man's eyes changed. A flicker—impossible to describe. As though a slide had been changed. And the eyes were different, and the face, the scowl, no longer seemed to be operated from something behind the man's skin.

This was the man, not the demon, and he stepped forward unhindered. Even as he did, the sword in April's hand grew less substantial—as though it might disintegrate from between her fingers. The demon was hiding itself.

But the man, and the gun, were very real.

"This is your chance," April said, licking her lips. "You can be free. We can set you loose now—the demon isn't in control."

"I heard what he told you," the man said in a voice that was far too pleasant, but which had also changed—this was not the same speaker as before. "He told you the truth. I want him here. We have not been coerced into the hive."

"Who are we? How many are you? Where are you?"

"Why don't you come and see?" the man asked. "Oh, no, that won't work. You are not to live beyond this afternoon. You, on the other hand," he looked at Diane again, "are cordially invited to come with me. I would not recommend turning down the invitation."

"Why don't I think I have an option?" Diane asked.

"Oh, you have an option. But you should know the ramifications. Come with me, and you will learn what you want to know. Don't come with me, and I will send a message to the hive and they will kill your son."

Her face went white, and he smiled.

"Yes, we have him. The other boy too, and those twins you sent after us."

He cocked the gun and held it at April's head, but with a half-playful expression that suggested he was only testing positions. "Where is the child?" he asked.

"Who?"

Without warning, he flipped the gun in his hand, strode forward, and clubbed April across the cheekbone with the butt. The blow knocked her sideways, and she sank halfway to the floor, hands shielding her face, but said nothing. He grabbed her arm and yanked her back up, shoving the barrel of the gun against her temple.

"Let me ask that question again. Where is the boy?"

A sound from behind him alerted him to Diane's presence, and he called out, louder than necessary, "Try anything, madam, and your son will die. I assure you, right now his life is in the balance. We will not kill him unless you give us reason to."

He brandished the gun again. April winced. Her eyes were closed, her teeth clenched. Her body shook, but she stayed on her feet. And said nothing.

"Heroics aren't going to accomplish anything," the man said. "If the boy is here, I'll find him. He won't escape me. Just tell me, save me a little time, and I'll make this a little easier on you."

April's eyes opened, and she looked past the man to Diane. She stood directly behind him, a butcher knife from the kitchen counter in her hand. But her expression was stricken, and she was frozen in place.

Do something, April's heart cried.

But what?

Kill him? Get blood on your hands? Provoke him to kill Chris?

No, she couldn't ask for that. For any of it.

And thought she knew, with sinking certainty, that Diane would not trade Chris's life for April's anyway.

"Was it you?" April asked. Her breath barely came enough to give her voice, but she managed to ask the question.

To stall.

"What are you talking about?"

"The highway murders. Did you kill those men?"

The man's eyes glimmered. "Oh, no, that was my brother. Bit of a loose cannon. But they backed him into a corner. He was transporting Chris and Tyler at the time."

"He didn't use a gun," April said, eyeing the cold steel up against her face.

Stupid, to push like this. Lunacy.

But maybe it would work.

"Of course not," the man growled. "He used his bare hands. Would you like me to demonstrate?"

"You can't. You need the demon's strength for that, and he's hiding."

The man snarled. He pulled the gun away from April's face and shoved her toward the kitchen door. She lost her balance and sprawled on the floor, grateful for every second, for every possible moment that he could misstep.

But how far would Richard's shield extend?

The man came for her, to grab her arm and shove her outside, but movement from beyond the window caught his eye, and he cursed. He took hold of her arm and yanked her to her feet, but this time he shoved her further into the house, into the common room behind the kitchen.

Deeper into the shield.

He kept the gun on her. "Get behind the couch," he said, following her as she obeyed. He cast another glare at Diane—who had somehow hidden the knife, or put it down. "Not one word. Try nothing. Anything you do, your son will pay."

The kitchen door bashed open. April couldn't see, from behind the couch, who was here. Her face felt like it had been split open, except that she couldn't feel blood. The man had fit himself behind the couch as well, his long legs folded up, the gun still trained straight on her.

Stall, she told herself. Keep stalling.

     Rachel Starr Thomson

Somehow, turn time so it's on your side.

It took her a moment to recognize the voice in the kitchen. A woman's voice.

Shelley.

Nick's mother.

"Where?" she was demanding in near-hysterics. "Where is he? His car is outside; he has to be here!"

"He's . . . he's not available right now," Diane said, her tone as motherly and as forceful as she could make it.

"Don't you give me that! She said you would protect my son! April said so! She lied to me! You people bring him here and then call that . . . that snake . . . that . . ."

She let off a stream of expletives.

"We're not handing Nick over to him," Diane insisted. "Yes, he's here, but we didn't invite him. We are protecting your son. April wouldn't lie to you."

"Well, where is he? And where's Nick?"

"Nick is safe."

"Where is he?"

April kept her eyes trained on the man, trying not to let Shelley's distress distract her. If this was a demon in control, if it wasn't being held back by Richard's shield, Shelley wouldn't be enough to break its concentration. It would just feed off of her.

But this was a man. A man who could get nervous, distracted, knocked off balance because the timing was wrong, because things weren't going as planned.

Her heart gathered up the surroundings, the voices, the pitched tension, and offered it in prayer. One word.

Please.

Shelley's hysteria grew louder; from behind the couch it sounded like her screams could be heard by the neighbours. And then she was threatening: "You tell me! You tell me or I'll call the police! I'll scream my head off and get everybody on the street in here! You just see if I don't!" There were sounds like a scuffle, and Diane yelping and Shelley yelling, "You stay out of my way!"

And then she was in the common room, hysterical, yelling into the house, "Where are you? You get out here and face me, you two-faced . . ."

And he lost it. The man rose to his feet, pointing the gun at her, hand shaking.

"Shut up, woman!" he said. "Keep your damn voice down before I shoot your throat out."

She went white at the sight of the gun.

April said a prayer. A reaching out to Diane. Broadcasting a thought and desperately hoping the air could truly carry it. Now.

One eye was swelling, half-shut, and adrenaline made her shake so hard she wasn't sure she could move, but in the split second that he stood and turned his attention to Shelley, she called the sword to hand and plunged it into his back.

He screamed, twisted, and dropped to his knees. The gun went off. Shelley likewise screamed, but in Diane's arms—Diane had heard, somehow, she had come. She had pushed Shelley out of the way at exactly the right moment.

In the narrow space between the couch and the wall, the man

     Rachel Starr Thomson

was trapped. April got up on his back, knees pinning his shoulders down, all of her weight concentrating on the sword piercing between his shoulder blades as his whole body convulsed. She could feel the floor on the other side of his body. The sword cut clear through, fading at the edge where it met skin and flesh but no less real, no less holding, for all that.

A double-edged sword, an old song said, piercing to the dividing asunder of soul and spirit, of bone and marrow.

A gurgling noise came from the man's throat, and a viscous substance began to appear on the floor, leaking from his mouth and eyes. It was dark, and it gathered itself on the floor like oil, not like water that spreads and dissipates.

Diane and Shelley both appeared over them, eyes wide.

"What is that, what's . . ."

"It's not anything you would understand," Diane said firmly. "Or want to."

"Him." Shelley pointed a shaking finger at the man on the floor, the man through whose back April was still holding a sword as firmly as she could while he shuddered and shook, twitching and trying unsuccessfully to buck her off. "He's a con man. He's worse than a con man. I found out about him . . . I saw his picture in a paper. He lied to me. He's no doctor. And he don't help kids. He's been up on charges of abuse and kidnapping and dealing." Her voice trailed away as she continued to stare at whatever was pooling on the floor. "But that . . ."

"I don't understand," Diane said, trying to meet April's eyes. April's jaw was clenched, and she hadn't moved. "When Reese and I fought demons, they just . . . left. One stab and they were gone."

"The hosts weren't hanging on to them," April explained through clenched teeth.

"That's why this is so hard? He doesn't want the demon to go?"

"That's why."

"Can you make it go anyway?"

"It's going." April nodded toward the puddle on the floor.

"It looks so hard."

April nodded again. "He might die. If he won't let go. The demon might just kill him anyway, but it can't—not under the shield. It's powerless. This is all him—the man. Hanging on if it kills him."

Fighting to stay in darkness.

Fighting to remain enslaved.

April found herself wishing he would die. Easier to deal with. Easier to explain that to the police, and go to trial and plead self-defense, than watch someone fight so hard to stay connected to so much nothingness, so much evil.

He choked out something, and then her wish came true.

He lay still.

He wasn't breathing.

She knew, although she couldn't feel it, that his heart had stopped.

She licked her lips and stood, slowly. "Call the police," she said.

"What?"

"He's dead. We're going to have to explain it. Better just call the police."

Diane laid a hand on April's arm. She looked up at the older woman, and neither said a word.

Diane let go and turned to the kitchen to make a phone call.

Shelley stood in the middle of the living room and said, "Nick."

Dread building in her heart, April turned. Nick was standing in the doorway toward the stairs. Just staring.

"How much . . . did you see that?" April asked. Heart breaking.

He stared.

And then he turned around and ran. Up the stairs. She heard feet pounding across the floor and the window being thrown open and knew he was out on the roof, and in a minute he'd be down the drainpipe, and then he'd be running, running toward the harbour.

Her face was throbbing. She could hardly see out of her left eye.

"Thank you," Shelley said. "Thank you for saving me. And my kid."

I didn't, April answered silently. I haven't even begun to save you. And I don't know what I just did to Nick.

"I'm sorry I said you were a liar," Shelley went on. "You done a whole lot for us. I'm sorry."

Wait, April's mind told her. Stop. Think. You can't talk to the police right now.

Why?

You have to find Chris.

We can't.

Yes, you can. You know where to go.

She struggled to understand what her own mind was telling her. Or perhaps it was the Spirit speaking. She didn't know if she could tell the difference just now. But April's gift—eyes to see. She had seen something. What?

"The car." The words came out her mouth before she'd even really thought about them. "Diane, the car!"

Diane appeared in the kitchen doorway, frowning. "What about it?"

"The license plate. We can trace it. We can find out where it comes from. The hive, Diane. We can trace the car back to the hive, and find Chris."

It was a tenuous hope, and she knew it. But it was the best they had.

Diane was still staring at the dead man on the floor. "What about him? We can't just leave him here."

"Did you call the police?"

"Not yet. I . . . I just couldn't yet."

"I don't know." April wrestled with herself, more torn than she wanted to admit. What she'd said to Diane was true. They had to get the police involved. Make sure they told their story— that the man had broken into their house and attacked them, then died of a heart attack—before they could be made to look guilty. But all of that would take time. And there would be

     Rachel Starr Thomson

questions, and maybe suspicions, and statements to be made, and limits to where they could go or what they could do until it was all over. And dealing with all of that meant not going after Chris and Tyler, not hunting down the hive. Not until too much time had passed.

For one fleeting instant April let herself hope that this man, dead on the floor, was it. There were no others; he was the only threat, and he was dead. The boys were safe.

She knew better.

But what choice did they really have?

In the end it was Shelley who clinched it for her. Nick's mother had slid down with her back to the wall and was staring at the dead man where his feet protruded from behind the couch, staring and moaning. They couldn't leave her like this. And they couldn't take her with them.

The Spirit knew that.

And the Spirit had sent her here. If it wasn't for Shelley, they wouldn't have had the opening they needed—the distraction necessary to get the upper hand.

And then, too, there was Nick. Someone needed to go after Nick.

"Call the police," April said. "We need to deal with this. But the car—while we're waiting for them, we can find out about the license plate."

"It's not going to do us any good if we can't go out and find the place," Diane said.

"We'll call Reese and Richard and Mary. Give them the info and let them track it down. They'll still be at the number

Richard traced—I hope."

"It's my son out there."

"Yes, I know." April met Diane's eyes with compassion. It was true. It was her son out there—her son being threatened.

And maybe that meant it was best Diane not go.

Maybe that was just one more piece of this particular plan.

She remembered asking Reese: "Do you think plans are real? Or is that just what we call something after everything has already happened and we can't imagine it going any other way?"

She still didn't know the answer to that, not for sure.

Today, like so many days, all she could really do with that uncertainty was trust.

     Rachel Starr Thomson

Reese got off the phone with a grim look and relayed everything April had told her about the twins' disappearance, Alex's drawings, the attack at the house, and the demonized attacker's cryptic threats toward Chris. Her news didn't send them in a new direction: they had already decided to head toward Brass. Miranda's story had told them nothing about how to find their friends; Reese gave the police all the information she had and let them set to work trying to find the moving van or the identity of the young man Miranda called Clint. Their only sure link to the hive was the teenage boy, Alex.

So they were heading back to Dr. Smith's.

Reese had installed the twins at the children's home to keep an eye on Alex partly because they didn't want to force the issue—to hurt the boy in the process. But now three men were dead, April had come a hair's breadth from being shot in the head, and Miranda had confirmed that the hive had Chris and Tyler. They were out of options.

Before they got off the phone, Reese assured April that talking to the police was the right thing to do. Like it or not, the law was tangled up in this, and so far the partnership had not been a bad one. Following up on that herself, Reese found Lieutenant Jackson and told him that a friend had been attacked up in the village and that he should know they thought the attacker was connected to the death of Rick Brodie, the murders on the highway, and the disappearance of their friends.

On their way now, she sat in brooding silence in the backseat of Richard's car. Mary watched her worriedly while Richard kept his eyes on the road, waiting for her to speak.

"We're missing something," she said finally.

"By which you mean . . ."

"What are they doing? What are they trying to do? This isn't all random. It's organized, much better organized than demons on their own ever are. But what is it? What are they trying to do to us? We're just reacting to them—letting them lead. We have no idea what they want. This isn't the way to fight a war."

"We know what they want," Mary said. "Destruction. Chaos."

"The demons want that. But they aren't alone. What does the hive want—the hive, together? And why are they coming after us?"

"We're their enemies."

"Yes, always have been and always will be. But I've been fighting demons most of my life, and they don't like to come after us. They like to terrorize vulnerable people, and get into their heads, and bring a lot of darkness. They don't often tangle with Oneness unless we go after them. Why are they hunting us?"

Richard was listening intently. "Keep talking, Reese," he said.

"Think about it. They attacked me—David did. Then they came after April—the killing cave. And they tried to kill all of you in the warehouse."

"All except Diane," Mary said.

Reese froze.

"What is it?" Mary asked, twisting around in her seat to get a better look at Reese. "Reese, what is it?"

"Diane."

"What about her?"

"Why is the hive bothering with Chris? Why in the world kidnap someone like him? And use him as a pawn? He's exactly the kind of person demons try to leave alone. He's not Oneness. He's not on the demon's side. He's much, much safer just to leave alone—to not push. So why have they kidnapped him?"

"You have a guess," Mary said.

"Yes. They want Chris for the same reason they started going after the village cell in the first place. To get to Diane."

"That doesn't really make sense," Mary responded. "When April disappeared, we realized they were targeting her because she's a great saint—because there's more power in her than any of us realized."

"She is that," Reese agreed, "and it's probably why the demons were too cowardly just to kill her. It's why the cave. But it's not why they targeted her in the first place."

"Well then?"

"Think about it. Think about where the hive is stemming from. Where it gets its power and its vision."

"From David," Richard said.

"Yes, from David. From a man who can't even be possessed because he's Oneness. And now there's Miranda . . . that man, Jacob. He's Oneness too."

"And yet he's operating outside of the Oneness," Mary said. "Acting more like a demon."

"To put it bluntly, yes."

"David is doing what he's doing because of the massacre when you were young. Because he lost everything he loved and decided to quit loving. I don't know what Jacob's story is, but I imagine it's similar—that there's a reason he's turned against the Oneness, or else decided he's its only true representative. That Clint guy must be connected to David somehow, and David's sent him to target Jacob. Why?"

"Ultimately," Mary said slowly, "so that the hive can spread through Jacob's community. That's how they usually work, isn't it? Capitalizing on already existing human networks?"

"Yes, exactly. So think. Think why Chris. Think why Diane."

The answer hit them all at once, and Richard groaned slightly.

"Because she's vulnerable," Mary said finally. "Because if Chris got hurt, she might still turn against us. Become another Jacob. Another David."

"They originally thought that taking out her cell would get to her; that's why they launched the initial attack on you, through April. But now they're striking closer to home."

"That's terrifying," Richard said.

"What is?" Mary asked.

"Think about their goals. What they want, ultimately. How they spread. To take the world into darkness through madness and control—the ultimate paradox. They use human networks to do it."

He allowed his eyes to leave the road for a split second, meeting Mary's. "There is no greater human network than the Oneness itself."

Mary gasped.

"That's what they're trying to do?"

"I think so," Reese said, bleakly.

"Is that even possible?"

"David turned. Jacob turned. Diane . . . Diane could turn. If their influence grew enough, reached out far enough, hurt enough of us . . ." Her voice trailed away.

"What about you, Reese?" Richard asked.

She closed her eyes. Not startled at the question—only hurt, and expectant. "What about me?"

"Are you vulnerable?"

"Why would you ask that?" Mary asked, shooting Richard a glare. But he ignored her.

"I'm not whole anymore," Reese said. "Not since what David did to me. I'm trying to come back, but . . ."

She was quiet a moment more. "I thought forgiveness would fix it. I thought when I forgave David and let him go, we had won. I had won. But I'm not whole. If something else happens . . ."

Her voice grew so quiet they could hardly hear it.

"If Chris dies."

"Finish that 'if,' Reese," Richard said.

"I don't know. I don't know what I would do. How I would be."

"Why us?" Mary whispered. "We're so small. Just one little cell in the middle of nowhere. Why would something this big start with us?"

"Because it doesn't have to be bigger. Because they can get into the Oneness one at a time. They already are."

Richard groaned again, and something in Reese snapped. She hit the side of the car with her fist and swore, and started to weep.

Mary looked helplessly at Richard.

"We need to find Chris," he said quietly. "I don't know what else we can do. But we've got to make sure that boy doesn't die. His mother depends on it. Reese depends on it." His voice dropped even lower. "Maybe we all do."

* * * * *

It was dark, incredibly so. Tyler didn't know how long they waited in the darkness. They'd been taken into a basement where the walls, the floor and the ceiling were painted black; there were no windows, no lights, only air that was damp, smelling of mildew and asbestos, and oppressive. The very air felt toxic, for spiritual reasons as much—or more than—as for physical.

They were not tied up or restricted in any way, just dumped on the concrete floor and left. Bonds would have been useless; they still couldn't move.

He knew Chris was there from the sound of his breathing, but they did not speak to each other. Tyler was not sure he could speak. He suspected the drugs—or poison, whatever it was—were affecting their vocal cords now.

In a way, that was a relief. He didn't know what he would say if he could talk. Or what Chris would say. Things were so far past hopeless that giving voice to them could only make everything feel worse. He hadn't even had a chance to fight. They'd been injected and lost before they could begin.

The images—his own imagination of the things he had not seen, but had heard and smelled—played over and over and over in his mind.

Upstairs, people were talking. The timbre of their voices carried down, but none of their words. He thought to himself, They're going to win, but the words hardly meant anything. He had seen them win. Had heard and smelled their winning. Carnage, chaos. Blood and senseless, senseless death.

He knew that ceding that—that it was all senseless, that it didn't fit a plan, that the policemen did not have to die but did anyway, just because some barely-more-than-a-child filled with some supernatural power killed them—was giving them a victory too. Oneness believed in meaning. In plans. In a Spirit holding everything together and ensuring that nothing was meaningless.

He had believed that.

Not anymore.

In this room, in this dark place, Tyler was ten again and his parents were dead, and people you should be able to trust—people like Jacob, who had the strength and the charisma to lead you, were your betrayers. The Oneness was not strong enough, or not real enough, to fill the howling void created by all that was wrong and crumbling away in the world. And he just had to deal with it, in the only way anyone ever could: by dying, by giving up forever.

A fleeting thought of Nick came to him, a small boy throwing himself off the end of a dock because he just couldn't take life anymore, because he wanted to swim away from it all.

You can't, Tyler thought, it finds you. It finds you and you just have to die. You can't even figure anything out before you do.

It was good that he couldn't talk to Chris. Couldn't voice any of this nihilism that was all he really thought or felt right now.

Upstairs, things went quiet, and then the whole atmosphere sank into a deeper, more twisted and perverse darkness. Tyler thought he could feel the ground throbbing beneath him and something filthy in the air. He could not move, thanks to the drugs, even to shudder. But his whole being quaked inside. In his mind's eye he went through it all again: the killings on the highway. The crunch of gravel under tires as the truck pulled off the road, his exultation and satisfaction at the sound of the police approaching. Their captor swearing. The truck door being raised, letting in blinding light.

          Rachel Starr Thomson

And then the killings.

Why he and Chris were still alive, he had no idea. What they wanted with them. What they had in mind to do with them.

Whatever was going on upstairs ceased, and the atmosphere normalized again—as normal as it could be down here. Then the door at the top of the stairs opened, letting in light, and two bodies came crashing down the stairs and landed in a heap at the bottom.

The twins.

They didn't move.

Again the door opened, and a skinny, unimposing figure appeared on the steps. He held up a flashlight and shone it down, into Tyler's eyes, and said in a voice that cracked with youth, "Where's the rest? You said we'd get all of 'em."

"They're coming," answered another voice, far too familiar. The young man in the moving truck. The Wizard, the hitch-hiker, the man without a name who spoke with a faint European accent and tore grown men apart with his bare hands and with glee. "My brother has shot the girl by now and is bringing the mother back with him. It has already begun."

"You're very confident," said another voice, one Tyler remembered too well even though he had been around it very little. David. His blood ran cold at the knowledge that this man was here too, and he wanted to cry and scream and maybe kill him. David's betrayal of the Oneness cut deeper than Tyler could explain, even now that he hardly believed in the Oneness anymore.

"I have every reason to be confident."

"They are stronger than they look, this cell. They've beaten us before."

"Correction, my friend. They have beaten you before, and that because you are too personal, too closely connected to them."

"They fought an entire core and won."

"Only after you had allowed it be fractured. You weakened, and your loss of strength tore the whole unit apart. You know the demons. It takes strength to hold them together. More strength than it seems you have."

David's voice had lowered dangerously. "You speak pretty strongly for someone who wouldn't even belong to this collective if it wasn't for me. The hive exists because of me."

"And it will go on existing without you, if it comes to that. You are not even possessed. You cannot be. That makes you the weaker."

"And you are an arrogant idiot," David replied. "You don't know anything about strength."

The Wizard laughed. "I killed two men with my hands. I think I know a great deal."

"You know what an animal knows. Mine is the mind driving this hive. Mine is the vision directing it."

"You are the god, yes, I know," the younger man said, but his tone was mocking.

The door closed and the teenager on the stairs disappeared behind it. The basement was plunged back into total darkness.

Tyler strained to hear anything from the twins—any sign

     Rachel Starr Thomson

of movement, any sound of breathing. He could hear nothing. Possibly they were already dead, and this basement was the crypt where they'd been buried.

He wondered who "the girl" was the Wizard said had been shot. Reese? April? "The mother" had to be Mary . . . or Diane.

He had just accepted that the twins were in fact dead when one of them moved. He wanted to call out to them, but he still could not speak.

Pray.

The word, the command, came at him out of the darkness as though spoken by a voice. Demanding obedience.

If he could have shaken his head, even his fist, at that voice, he would have done it. He had seen the futility of prayer. He had seen the futility of believing in anything except chaos and death.

Pray.

He found that although no other part of him could move, he could close his eyes. Tightly. He did so. Willing the very idea away from him.

Pray.

Why? his spirit shouted back. What good does it do? What good does anything do? It's not enough! Prayer is not enough. The Oneness is not enough. The Spirit, whatever the Spirit is, is not enough. All there is is emptiness, lack, horror, and dying.

All that fighting does is exhaust you.

For a moment his mind settled into a weary rest, as though the voice had waited for him to say his piece and was letting him calm himself before it spoke again.

And then there it was again.

Pray.

No use, Tyler argued, more weakly this time. This is me we're talking about. Me. I can't tell the difference between a demon-controlled maniac and a Spirit-filled leader of the Oneness. I can't tell when a warehouse is full of demons or if my fellow Oneness, only a few feet away from me, are dead or alive. I can't pray. I'm not enough. I've never been enough.

The voice answered: You are not alone.

Pray for what, how? He wondered. He wished he was Richard. Richard knew how this worked. Richard could—

The answer cut off his own thoughts, surprising him. He'd thought he was talking to himself. But his own voice wouldn't invade quite like this, would it?

Reach out.

I can't even move.

Reach out.

A tiny, almost imperceptible sigh escaped him.

He pictured Richard. Concentrated, tried to see the older man's face. His wise eyes and his gentle smile, and the authority with which he spoke. That was something you could picture, intangible though it was. Authority marked every line on Richard's face. And then Mary. He pictured her too. He started by trying to see her face as he knew it, but for some reason the image kept morphing, showing him a younger woman instead. The woman who had known David in his early years, who had brought him into the Oneness. The woman who had come to the village fleeing from an attack much like this one, and had brought Diane into the Oneness too, and eventually brought April home.

He tried to picture April then, and was momentarily stopped when he remembered that she might be dead. A lump came into his throat, and his heart beat harder, but he forced the feelings back and just pictured her. Of all the village Oneness, he knew April least. Yet she was part of him. As he pictured he could feel her strength, her courage, her compassion reaching out to him. He felt it and thought she could not be dead.

But that thought made him picture Patrick, who was dead—or wasn't, as was the case in the cloud. Patrick who had appeared several times to him while he was still outside the Oneness and then again when he was in, talking to him and assuring him there was a plan, there were reasons for everything, and proving beyond argument that death just was not the end Tyler had always assumed it was.

He pictured Reese, fiery, tormented, strong-willed Reese.

He formed Diane in his mind's eye, his surrogate mother.

He reached out, in spirit, for the twins. He found that when he did, they were not dead or even unconscious or even trapped; they were vibrant and strong as ever, full of life, full of ideas and bravery and ready for anything. He almost smiled, both at the image of the twins and at his own hubris in imagining them like that.

Pray, the voice had said. Was this prayer? Was he actually accomplishing anything but thinking of all these who were part of him and smiling at thoughts of their strength and their humanity and their companionship?

Something wet hit his shoulder and trickled down his arm.

The sensation was incredibly irritating, and he wished more than anything he could wipe it off. He still couldn't move. Another drip, another trickle. Slow and heavy.

For a terrifying moment he thought it might be blood, but then he smelled it.

Kerosene.

His hair stood on end.

More drops, hitting his hair and face and shoulders and hands and feet. Sprinkling like rain from overhead. His skin was crawling even as he wanted to gag on the smell. He knew what they were doing. Preparing the pyre. Drenching the sacrifice.

They were going to burn the house and everyone in it.

He could hear noise upstairs, scuffling, raised voices.

And then there were tears on his face again, mingling with the fuel.

Reach out.

For one more person.

For Chris.

Two more—Chris, and Nick.

They weren't One. Weren't even reachable like the others were. But Tyler reached for them anyway. Desperately tried to find their spirits in the dark, picture their faces, join strength with them both and pull them home to safety.

He wasn't sure exactly when the Oneness had begun to feel safe again.

But in a sudden, hazy blaze of light, as though he was seeing

 Rachel Starr Thomson

through smoke to a brightly lit room, he saw Patrick, and many others, and beings he thought might be angels, all standing in the basement with them and driving a message home.

Never alone.

Never, never alone.

Never, ever, ever alone.

Tyler believed it. The scene vanished. The kerosene fell faster. He did gag on the smell.

* * * * *

Richard pulled his car to a stop directly behind the moving truck, and they piled out without fanfare. Hilts throbbed in their hands, but they held the swords back, not yet giving them form. The air stank of witchcraft and smelled also of blood. The latter smell, they guessed, came from the moving truck.

Reese marched to the front door and pounded on it.

They wanted a fight, they were going to get one. No sneaking in this time. No lurking around the edges, biding their time. There was no time to bide.

The air shifted, tinting itself a different colour, and the wood grain of the door began to swirl as the physical makeup of the world around them started to re-form.

"None of that!" Richard boomed.

His voice returned the world to normal.

Spell stymied.

Reese pounded on the door again.

It was thrown open from within, and she found herself facing a woman she had never seen before. The woman was about thirty, professional, harried. She appraised Reese with a barely hidden sneer.

"Yes?" she said. "Who are you, and what do you want?"

"You don't really need to ask that, do you?" Reese answered.

"This is my house," the woman answered. "I think you owe me an explanation of why you're trying to take my door off its hinges."

"You wouldn't be Mrs. Smith, would you?" Reese asked.

The woman flushed. Identified.

But that thought stopped Reese in her tracks. "Wait, where are the children?" she asked.

Behind her, Mary and Richard had been drawing closer to the door, but they stopped. "What children?"

"April said there were children," Reese said, ignoring the woman who still stood in the doorway. "When the fake Dr. Smith came for Nick, he had a 'wife' and two children with him. April just took out the doctor. Here's the wife. Where are the children?"

The woman snarled, with an expression so animalian that Reese drew back. The snarl resolved into a smile, just as terrifying.

"Why don't you come in and see?" she said. "For that matter, I think a few of your friends are here already. They'd love for you to join the party."

   Rachel Starr Thomson

Reese stayed where she was, tensed with indecision. Her first instinct had been to let the sword form in her hand and drive the demon out of this woman, no matter what the results be to her. The Oneness never took a human life if they could help it, but war was war, and if people were going to involve themselves to this degree, their lives couldn't be guaranteed on either side. But the thought of the children had thrown her off. Kill this woman, she could maybe do. Especially after April had already killed someone earlier this same day. But she couldn't be responsible for the deaths of children, and there was a good chance there were two—or more—in this house.

She thought of Miranda and the children's home and nearly was sick. If the hive's first goal was to turn the Oneness against itself and use their influence in the world to spread possession and demonic control, children were among their prime targets. Oneness could not be possessed, but people working alongside demons could be just as bad as people possessed by them, and perhaps more able to target the innocent.

"What do you think, we're holding them hostage?" the woman said, pleasure glowing in her eyes. "Or are you just afraid to come in and find out that children are on our side too?"

"No child is on your side," Reese said. "Even if you have gained control of them."

"Naive," the woman said.

"We want to see our friends," Reese said. "You can let us in and let them go, peacefully, or there can be a fight. And I will wager we're stronger than you are."

The woman laughed. "Not one for subtlety, are you? Do you always go marching into battle like you're going to destroy the whole enemy army at one go? Didn't learn much from the warehouse fight. We are always in more places than you think. We always have plans you don't know about."

Reese flushed, the shame and pain of the battle where she had lost Patrick and invited the distrust and exile of David's cell coming back. The woman's comment bit deep, deeper than the words themselves should allow. She knew the powers in the air were playing on her emotions and dredging up the exile to throw her off, keep her from being strong enough or clear-headed enough to make good decisions in the moment. Chris had once told her grief was dangerous. She wrestled her mind back to focus, trying to ignore the pain forcing its way up her throat.

"Let us in," she said quietly, "and we'll see who is ready for who."

She stepped forward, and to her surprise, the woman stepped back and motioned for her to enter the open door.

Second thoughts raced through her mind. The woman's words plagued her. This wasn't wise. Richard and Mary should have gone around the back and tried to get in some other way. They should have gone to the Lincoln cell to try and get more help. They should have tried to draw the hive leaders out into neutral territory, tried to take this more slowly. This was the warehouse all over again, and once again, she was leading the way into disaster.

She swallowed all of that fear and stepped inside the house.

The entrance was a dingy foyer with old, stained carpet and striped, wallpapered walls. A living room, empty, was shadowed off to one side. The place felt old and smelled like mildew and something else. A strong, dirty smell with a physical impact.

Some kind of gas.

Instantly, she felt herself on intensified alert. The heightened awareness brought on by the smell also linked her more strongly to the man and woman following her, and she felt the rush and fear attendant upon Mary's own memories. There had been something about an explosion in her history, Reese knew. Death by fire.

But they stepped in behind her. And now all swords were drawn and fully visible.

The possessed woman stood five feet in front of them, in front of a doorway into another room. If anyone else was in the house, they weren't showing themselves. The air felt stretched, tense, but no demonic presence was visible but the one dwelling inside this human being.

She was so normal, so much a woman—a mother, a wife, a daughter. Short, styled hair; stylish clothing; well-kept nails. And something inhuman looking out through her eyes.

"What are you waiting for?" that something asked. "You're here to battle, aren't you? Drive me out."

Reese clenched her fingers more tightly around the hilt.

"Come on," the demon taunted. "Of course you might kill her, but you knew that when you came here. If you don't risk killing her, you'll lose your friends and your lives. We will win because you didn't even try to stop us."

Reese took a step forward.

"Her name is Hilary," the demon announced. "She was born in Lincoln. Went to college out east, got married, went through a painful divorce. She likes movies and walking on the beach.

She's spent hours by the ocean, crying or reading or trying to find some meaning and hope in this life."

Reese stopped. She couldn't do this. She knew she was playing into the demon's game, but she couldn't just plunge a sword into this woman knowing what would happen to her. It was bad enough she had almost killed Alex in the schoolyard. Then, she had just been trying to get information—she hadn't intended to keep going until he died. But here, that choice wasn't part of the equation. It was drive the demon out, probably killing its hostess in the process, or leave all the advantage in the enemy's hands.

The demon smirked. "What? Can't bring yourself to admit that there is no hope, no meaning? That death is the only way?"

From behind the woman, two figures stirred in the next room and slowly padded out, eyes glassy. Children. A boy and a girl. They walked past Reese, totally ignoring her, and each took one of Richard's hands and held them. Staring straight forward. His sword disintegrated. He couldn't hold it and their hands at the same time, and he wouldn't hurt them.

Reese turned her head enough to see, and she groaned inside. Richard was incapacitated from a fight unless he could find a way to get the children out of harm's way. Little chance of that, considering they were possessed. Mary, still armed, looked from Richard to Reese. Her expression showed the strain she was under.

The smell of gas was getting stronger.

Another figure moved into place. Reese had been wrong: the shadowy living room wasn't empty. A young man wearing all black, with a thick head of blond hair and smile that was pure mockery, stood in the doorway and held up both hands. Arcane

   Rachel Starr Thomson

symbols were tattooed on both palms.

And his fingernails were ruddy with blood.

The spirit of murder was so strong in his presence that Reese almost choked on it. Murder and witchcraft.

He beckoned slightly with one hand.

"Come," he said, his voice slightly accented. "Come to the fight you are so eager for."

"Where are Chris and Tyler?" she asked.

"Come and see."

She knew better.

She knew better than to answer the demons' taunt, than to step forward when they said step forward. She knew better, even though she kept doing it. She knew better, but she had no choice. They held all the cards.

So she stepped forward.

Beneath her feet, the floor turned to mud and sucked her down, rug and floorboards buckling and then liquidating in a whirlpool of world turned wrong. A howling filled her ears, and she heard Richard shouting something, and she fell through.

The fall was sharp, quick, over as she hit concrete and heard the snap of a bone. Searing pain ran up her leg. Her sword gone, she rested her weight on both hands, but they threatened to slip away from her. The floor was slick with kerosene, the air choking with it, the whole room a pyre. Darkness suffocated any light; she could see nothing and hear only the drip, drip, drip of kerosene from above.

But she wasn't alone.

Tyler and the twins were here. She could feel them, knew they were alive, though no one moved or said anything.

She tried to pull herself forward, and in the process her hands found someone.

It only took a minute to realize it was Chris.

He was breathing, but his skin was cold, and he didn't respond to her presence. She found a cast on his arm and a bruise swelling the side of his face. But she knew that face, even only under her fingers. She had memorized it, without realizing she was doing it. She knew the jawline, the eyes, the mouth.

She didn't want him to die here.

Not just because it would be a setback in this war. Not just because it would put Diane at risk of turning. Not even just because it would put her at risk of turning.

She didn't want to lose him. She didn't want him to die without becoming Oneness, without knowing who she was in the deepest way and being known that way in return. And she didn't want to lose the future with him in it, whatever it might mean, whatever it might look like.

Chris was a pawn, a game piece in a game the demons were playing, and she hated it with every atom of her being.

Tears were streaming down her face as she positioned herself next to him, wrapping him in her arms.

Sometimes terrible things happened, and the Oneness would pull themselves together and call it a plan. They would say the Spirit directed and held all things together and nothing was meaningless, and because it was not meaningless there was an element to all things that was good, redemptive.

     Rachel Starr Thomson

Not to this.

The vehemence of her own belief frightened her, but she did not—would not—back down.

Chris's dying here was not a plan she would accept.

No matter the cost of unacceptance.

If that put her against the Spirit and the Oneness itself, so be it.

*   *   *   *   *

Mary backed up, standing alongside Richard, and struggled to keep her footing as the floor continued to swirl and morph into something it should not have been. The young man in the living room door laughed.

"That's enough," Richard said, quiet but stern. His hands were still held by the stone-faced children, and he did not move a muscle.

When he spoke, the boy shuddered from head to foot, shaking so hard that Richard found himself hanging on to the boy's hand instead of the other way, trying to comfort him and keep him standing.

The floor steadied and straightened, but the young man only grew taller in his arrogant assurance. "You don't think we did not prepare for you and your tongue? Speak again, and we will kill the children."

Richard closed his mouth.

The young man was not bluffing.

The children stared forward.

"You think you have such great power, with your words and your spirit life. But ours is the power of the earth and the air, and we are embraced by humans and made gods. You cannot even fight us. You are trapped by your loves and your unity."

"Then why do you want to emulate it?" Mary said, answering for Richard. "Why join yourselves in this monstrosity? Why seek any kind of unity at all?"

"It is useful," the man said, smiling. His face should have been handsome, the smile even more so, but with the demon speaking through him it only looked hideous.

Another figure in the other room stirred, and David appeared beside the young man.

Mary closed her eyes.

"You might as well face it, Mary," she heard him say. "I've anticipated everything. Reese's passion, Richard's mouth. Your dogged loyalty and unwillingness to hurt children—or even these others, who would only be hurt because they're hanging on so hard to their own demonic masters. This fight is over."

"And when we're dead?" Mary said. "Where will you go from there?"

"Oh, you won't all be dead. Richard, yes. You, probably. But I intend to bring Reese up from below before we burn this place down. A resurrection, if you like. Because I know that she will do what I did when I lost everyone I cared about in a demonic attack—in a fire. She will turn against the Oneness. I'm sorry Diane isn't here yet—I wanted her to see the fire and smell the smoke for herself. But I think seeing the remains will do it."

"And me? You're considering leaving me alive because you think you can turn me too?"

"Not really," David said. "But I can make you suffer. And I want to. Everything I have gone through—you were the reason for it all."

She opened her eyes and looked him full in his. "You haven't won everything. You meant to kill April, twice now, and you didn't. She's still alive. You lost the man you sent to shoot her."

She saw the faltering in his expression, but he didn't react. "Even a cat goes through its last life eventually."

"I'm sorry," Mary whispered. She cleared her throat, trying to force her voice to come out more loudly, more clearly. "I didn't wish this on you."

"It's too late now."

"It's not too late. It's never too late."

He laughed. "What, did you think Reese's letting me go was going to strike me to the heart? That I would repent and become a new man, undone by her kindness and love? Reese is a stupid girl. I want the release of death. I want to be released into chaos. But I refuse to die without taking as many of you down with me as I can."

He smiled bitterly. "After all, I am still Oneness. All for one, and one for all. Reese sins against me, I sin against you."

Mary could see the disdain in the eyes of the young man who still stood next to David, disdain and impatience. Patience, care, planning—these were not the demons' strong points.

Which was why, she realized in a flash of insight, David had indicated they would not wait for Diane to burn the house down—even though he had not known about the failure to kill April and bring Diane here. He could not contain the demonic in this house much longer. They wanted death, and they were going to get it.

She exchanged an anguished look with Richard. Mary had faced death before. She'd done it with courage and grace. Death was not the end for the Oneness.

But this time she felt little courage, no grace, no peace.

For one reason:

Chris.

A teenager appeared from the room where the children had been. He held up a shining light—an oil lamp, Mary saw, an old-fashioned lamp with glass panes and a burning wick. He wore all black, and his eyes were eager.

"Now?" he asked.

"All right," David said, keeping his eyes fixed on Mary. "In a minute. Clint, go get Reese."

* * * * *

Tyler heard it when Reese fell through the ceiling, and he felt her presence now, a throbbing, burning, pulsating flame. He felt her love and her fear and her anger, and the danger that surrounded her.

He swallowed hard, glad to find he had that much control over his muscles. Even before becoming Oneness, he had cared about Reese.

    Rachel Starr Thomson

In the dark, he could hear her crying.

He wished he could help.

You can, a voice told him.

I can't, he answered back. I can't even move.

He hated how weak he was.

The door upstairs opened and footsteps came down, silhouettes in the light from above. The Wizard and the kid. Reese tried to fight them off, but she couldn't.

"You can't win," the kid said, his adolescent voice cracking in his excitement. "We planned it all. You've all just walked right into the plans."

They disappeared again, the door shut, the darkness ruled.

Tyler still couldn't move.

The kid's words bothered him more than he could say. Plans—plans were supposed to be a thing of the Spirit. But in this case, the teen was right. They had planned everything. And the Oneness had just walked right into their plans.

The only thing that could beat them now, Tyler thought, is a surprise.

Like if I got up and walked out of here.

If I could do that, maybe I could do more. Because they wouldn't expect it. Because they think I can't move.

The power of the unexpected could win.

And he didn't know it was his own voice or the other one he kept hearing, the one that told him to do ridiculous things like pray, but he clearly heard the words, So do it.

I can't move! he reminded whoever it was.

So don't use your own strength.

The thought was like seeing a sun rise for the first time and suddenly knowing that you are a planet in relation to other orbs, and that the world that feels still under your feet is moving. As soon as it came, he knew it was possible.

He knew that the Oneness could move his body even while drugs were supposed to be paralyzing it.

He knew that it didn't matter how weak he was, because he had the strength of thousands of others.

I don't know how, he meekly offered.

But he was running out of time.

* * * * *

In the kitchen, beside the basement door, Alex and the demon inside him had neatly stacked two bales of dry straw, brought from Jacob's community farm. They would light easily and burn well, then burn down the trail of fuel under the door and down the steps until the fire hit the kerosene.

Alex's hands shook with anticipation, and he almost dropped the match. They'd planned it to give them all enough time to get out, but he almost wished he could stay here and walk in the fire like a demon himself. Only the ingloriousness of dying alongside the Oneness, almost like he was one of them, made him decide against the idea.

The Wizard would be able to walk through the fire and live,

but he was not as experienced or as full of demons as Clint. Yet.

He turned to take in the sight of the house, picturing it in flames, picturing the smoke, the heat, the walls peeling and ceilings collapsing and floors giving way in a roar of flame from beneath. He laughed.

His own laugh kept him from hearing the basement door behind him opening.

He turned to light the fire, and the demon inside him screamed out with rage.

* * * * *

"What's keeping him?"

A minivan in the garage had been pulled out, and they sat in the driveway with the engine running: David in the front passenger's seat, antsy and voicing it, the young man, Clint, beside him. In the middle bench Mary waited with the woman next to her. The empty seat next to her, beside the open van door, was for Alex. The children were huddled in the backseat.

Reese, wrists and ankles duct-taped and a blindfold pulled over her eyes, had been dumped in the back. Richard, unconscious, had been left inside.

"He's an idiot," Clint offered.

"I only gave him one job! What's taking him so long?"

"He'll do it. He's hungry for this."

Their eyes, all their eyes, were fixed on the front door of the house.

But Alex didn't show.

Finally David jumped out of the van and started pacing.

"Get back in," Clint said. "Someone will see you. The last thing you want is to draw attention to us now."

"Don't you tell me what to do!"

Mary found herself looking around, hoping someone would see them and come to inquire what was going on. But what was—

Tyler.

She felt him reach out for her and knew he was inside, alive, and active. Somehow, impossibly, he had stopped Alex from lighting the fire.

One of the children, the girl, let out a long, hopeless wail.

The woman turned on her, but Mary turned at the same time, and she saw. She saw the child looking out past the demonic sheen, the desperate plea for help.

Before today, these children had chosen their demons.

They weren't choosing them any longer. At least, this one wasn't.

Mary reached out without thinking, immediately grabbing the child's hand and speaking the words of release to one who had requested it. "You are heard! You are free!"

The woman turned on her in rage, but the damage was done. The demon left the child's body with a shriek. The little boy, at the same time, lurched forward and grabbed Mary's arm with both his hands. At first she thought it was an attack, that he was trying to stop her. But his eyes, again, told the story. She

    Rachel Starr Thomson

repeated the words. His demon let loose.

The woman reached out to grab Mary's throat and strangle her then and there, but the sword was already in her hand, and she pierced the woman through.

Her scream, of pain and anger and shock, shook the van.

Mary held the sword, driving it forward, driving the demon out, and prayed silently that the woman would not die. At any moment she expected Clint to stop her. Or David. How long could it take them to turn around, to get into position to do something, to respond?

The demon left her in a cloud of writhing smoke, and the woman collapsed. The children, scared, were crying. Mary looked at them. "Get down," she said. "Untie Reese and stay with her. She'll protect you."

She turned, one hand on the seat in front of her, the other hand holding her sword at the ready. Clint should be in that seat, should be fighting her.

He wasn't.

At some point between the first child's wail for release and the woman's collapse, he had exited the van and charged toward the house. He stood on the doorstep now, frozen in place, with a sword point at his throat.

Richard was on the other end of it.

And behind him, Tyler.

David stood in the midst of the yard, raging. He was shouting, but relief and triumph and the sudden flood of hope throbbing through Mary's ears drowned out his words completely.

And then something else was drowning him out.

Sirens.

Three police cars, one after the other, pulled up in front of the house. Lieutenant Jackson got out of the first one. Across the street, another car pulled up to the curb, and a man Mary suspected was the real Dr. Vincent Smith got out, followed by a woman who might have been his wife.

Her hands started to shake, and she felt the tears coming.

"Reese," she said. She turned . . . the children had managed to get Reese out of half her bonds, and the blindfold was gone. She was propped up against the side of the van, standing on one leg high enough for her head and shoulders to show above the backseat.

"That's Dr. Smith," Reese said, her voice full of emotion.

"I thought so."

"Did we save him?"

Him. Chris.

Mary smiled through her tears. "Yes, I think we did."

The cell house was quiet at midnight. Prayer was over, the police had gone. Mary sat at the dining room table, sipping a cup of tea and mulling.

Richard sat down next to her. She hadn't known he was still up, but she smiled wearily at him.

"I wish they were all home," she said.

"They will be soon. The boys just need to get those drugs out of their systems, and they'll let the twins out as soon as they can prove nobody got hit too hard in the head."

Mary nodded, holding the heel of her hand against her mouth. She removed it and sipped at her tea again, looking absently into the living room. It seemed unreal that April had killed a man in there earlier the same day. April, at least, had passed a medical examination and been allowed to come home right away. Nick had wandered in after ten, after dark, and said very little but shown tremendous relief to find April okay.

His mother was upstairs in one of the beds, but they didn't tell him that. He would find out in the morning.

To Mary's comfort, Diane had announced her intention to stay here tonight also. No going away to a home of her own—no leaving the family. She and Reese were still at the hospital in Lincoln, hovering around Chris's room, but they would be home soon.

The cell house had never been this full. And yet, Mary's heart would not truly quiet until they were all home, all safe, all here where she could see them and know they were okay.

It might not even truly quiet then.

"When . . . when they come home. It still won't be complete."

"You can't turn David's heart," Richard said. "How he is—it isn't your fault, Mary. He's made his own choices."

She nodded, but she kept her eyes distant, fixed on the door. She had already made arrangements to visit Julie and Miranda, the woman and her daughter from the community who had outed Jacob, and would try to visit Jacob himself, and his wife, as soon as they were allowed visitors. A court date hovered in their near future. What exactly the charges would be, no one knew yet.

Maybe, despite the wrongness of some of their actions, despite their opening the door to the hive, they weren't too far gone.

Maybe they weren't David. Yet.

"I know you just want to gather everyone and keep them safe," Richard said, slowly, obviously building to something.

      Rachel Starr Thomson

"I know I can't," she interrupted. "We're all soldiers. I understand."

"He's going to come after us again."

Mary shook her head, putting her cup down and resting her head in her hands. "No. No, we can't let him. We need to go after him this time. Reese was right all along. So was Chris. Defensive tactics don't work against this. They just have us dancing to whatever tune the demons play. We have to attack."

She looked at Richard with surprising calm. "I trust you're prepared for that."

"I will be," he said, the hint of a smile playing around his mouth.

"Good."

"Do you have a plan?"

"I will have." This time she did smile, and Richard chuckled.

"You know," he said, "Nick showed me some of his drawings. April is teaching him a lot."

Her smile faltered. "That boy, Alex, he drew too. Dr. Smith showed me."

"Artistic souls," Richard said. "They're drawn to spirit one way or another."

"Do you think the police can keep Clint and David and the rest in jail? That it will go all the way to a trial?"

"No," Richard said. "I think we'll learn that they all got away."

"Hopefully not at the cost of any more lives."

"We can't control that."

Mary nodded. "In the morning," she said, "call everyone together. We need to pray. And figure out what we're going to do."

A knock on the kitchen lintel made them both look up. "Mind if I join you?" April asked.

"Not at all." Richard moved his chair aside to make more room, and she sat. Weariness showed in every line of her face.

"I didn't know talking to police all day was so draining."

"I'm glad they didn't decide you needed to be brought in."

"They believed our story—we all told the same one. He came in and attacked us, and his death was an accident in the course of self-defense."

She smiled. "Shelley is the real hero. If she hadn't come when she did, it would have gone their way."

"Surprises," Mary said.

"What Tyler did was impossible," April said, half-question.

"So the ER doctor said. Those drugs were so strong, he shouldn't have been able to move until tomorrow. Talk, maybe, but not climb a set of stairs, drive a demon out of a teenager, and rouse Richard in time."

"What were you talking about?" April asked.

"What's about to happen."

"And that is . . .?"

Mary looked grim, but there was relief in her voice when she said the words.

 Rachel Starr Thomson

"We're going to attack."

* * * * *

It was way past visitor hours, but Reese snuck in and sat beside Chris's bed anyway. Tyler was on the other side of the room—the hospital had obliged Diane's pleas and put them together. He was asleep like the hero he was, enjoying well-deserved rest.

Chris was wide awake and looking at Reese, just gazing at her face as he held her hand. She tried to swallow the lump in her throat for the millionth time.

"You know I can't be with you, not like that, if you're not Oneness."

"You just told me you would have turned your back on the Oneness if I had died."

"Would you have wanted that?"

He was quiet for a moment. "No. I just can't come over and be one of you just because you, or Tyler, want me to."

"I just wish you could hear the call for yourself."

"Maybe I will. One day."

"Maybe you need to open your ears."

His grip on her hand grew tighter. "Reese, don't fight. Not right now. Just let me be glad to be alive and to be looking at your face and holding your hand."

She gripped back. "I'm glad too."

Diane, across the room at Tyler's bedside, said, "Time to go home."

Reese stood, and Chris reluctantly let go of her hand. In the dark, under the bed lamp, he gazed up at her.

"I'm coming home soon," he said.

She smiled, and didn't ask him to clarify.

* * * * *

The story continues in Book 3: ATTACK.

 Rachel Starr Thomson

Rachel would love to hear from you!

You can visit her and interact online:
Web: **www.rachelstarrthomson.com**
Facebook: **www.facebook.com/RachelStarrThomsonWriter**
Twitter: **@writerstarr**

The Seventh World Trilogy

Worlds Unseen   Burning Light   Coming Day

For five hundred years the Seventh World has been ruled by a tyrannical empire—and the mysterious Order of the Spider that hides in its shadow. History and truth are deliberately buried, the beauty and treachery of the past remembered only by wandering Gypsies, persecuted scholars, and a few unusual seekers. But the past matters, as Maggie Sheffield soon finds out. It matters because its forces will soon return and claim lordship over her world, for good or evil.

The Seventh World Trilogy is an epic fantasy, beautiful, terrifying, pointing to the realities just beyond the world we see.

"An excellent read, solidly recommended for fantasy readers."
– Midwest Book Review

"A wonderfully realistic fantasy world. Recommended."
– Jill Williamson, Christy-Award-Winning Author
of *By Darkness Hid*

"Epic, beautiful, well-written fantasy that sings of Christian truth."
– Rael, reader

Available everywhere online or special order from your local bookstore.

The Oneness Cycle

| Exile | Hive | Attack | Renegade | Rise |

*The supernatural entity called the Oneness holds the world together.
What happens if it falls apart?*

In a world where the Oneness exists, nothing looks the same. Dead men walk. Demons prowl the air. Old friends peel back their mundane masks and prove as supernatural as angels. But after centuries of battling demons and the corrupting powers of the world, the Oneness is under a new threat—its greatest threat. Because this time, the threat comes from within.

Fast-paced contemporary fantasy.

*"Plot twists and lots of edge-of-your-seat action,
I had a hard time putting it down!"*
—Alexis

"Finally! The kind of fiction I've been waiting for my whole life!"
—Mercy Hope, FaithTalks.com

"I sped through this short, fast-paced novel, pleased by the well-drawn characters and the surprising plot. Thomson has done a great job of portraying difficult emotional journeys . . . Read it!"
—Phyllis Wheeler, The Christian Fantasy Review

Available everywhere online or special order from your local bookstore.

Novels by Rachel Starr Thomson

Taerith

"Devastatingly beautiful" . . . "Deeply satisfying."

Lady Moon

"Laugh-out-loud funny"

*"Reminiscent of Patricia C. Wrede and
Terry Brooks's Magic Kingdom for Sale."*

Reap the Whirlwind

"Haunting."

Theodore Pharris Saves the Universe

"Imaginative and hilarious."

***Available everywhere online
or special order from your local bookstore!***

Short Fiction by Rachel Starr Thomson

Butterflies Dancing

Fallen Star

Of Men and Bones

Ogres Is

Journey

Magdalene

The City Came Creeping

Wayfarer's Dream

War With the Muse

Shields of the Earth

And more!

*Available as downloads for
Kindle, Kobo, Nook, iPad, and more!*